mr. terupt
falls again

Also by Rob Buyea

Because of Mr. Terupt

mr. terupt
falls again

ROB BUYEA

delacorte press

Text copyright © 2012 by Rob Buyea
Jacket art copyright © 2012 by Harry Bliss

All rights reserved. Published in the United States by Delacorte Press, an imprint of Random House Children's Books, a division of Random House, Inc., New York.

Delacorte Press is a registered trademark and the colophon is a trademark of Random House, Inc.

Visit us on the Web! randomhouse.com/kids

Educators and librarians, for a variety of teaching tools, visit us at RHTeachersLibrarians.com

Library of Congress Cataloging-in-Publication Data
Buyea, Rob.
Mr. Terupt falls again / Rob Buyea. —1st ed.
p. cm.
Summary: Several students relate their experiences helping Mr. Terupt move the old classroom to the sixth grade annex during the summer vacation.
ISBN 978-0-385-74205-4 (hc) — ISBN 978-0-375-98910-0 (ebook) —
ISBN 978-0-375-99038-0 (glb)
1. Classrooms—Juvenile fiction. 2. Moving, Household—Juvenile fiction.
3. Teacher-student relationships—Juvenile fiction. 4. Summer—Juvenile fiction.
[1. Classrooms—Fiction.   2. Moving, Household—Fiction.
3. Teacher-student relationships—Fiction.   4. Summer—Fiction.]
I. Title. II. Title: Mister Terupt falls again.
PZ7.B98316Mr 2012
[Fic]—dc23
2012010897

The text of this book is set in 12-point Goudy.
Book design by Kenny Holcomb

Printed in the United States of America

10 9 8 7 6 5 4 3 2 1

First Edition

To my wife and best friend, Beth,
whom I fell for long ago

PART ONE

summer

Peter

It was one of those farts that stunk so bad you could taste it. One of those that made your eyes water and forced you to tuck your nose under your shirt collar. It must have been hot and steamy coming out, because there's no other explanation for its horrid stench. I know, it sounds like your classic silent-but-deadly—it wasn't. Her fart ripped like a firecracker when it went off. That's right—it wasn't me! It was Lexie!

She dropped her stink bomb one day during the summer when we were helping Mr. T move our old classroom down to the sixth-grade annex. After last year, I wanted to spend all my time with Mr. T. I didn't want a day to go by that I wasn't with him. That's why I spent my vacation helping him with the move. Besides, Mom and Dad weren't around. They were working all the time—even in the summer, business called. And my older brother, Richard, was off doing his own thing, which was DJing. He had his own equipment and did small parties, birthdays mostly. It wasn't like we needed the money, and Mom and Dad didn't force him to get a job, but that's what he did. He said it helped him get the girls.

Lexie and I weren't the only ones choosing to hang with Mr. T. Anna and Ms. Newberry helped a lot, and Jeffrey showed up some, too. There weren't a lot of other people around school in the beginning, just our custodians, office staff, and our principal, Mrs. Williams.

I was on my way to our classroom one morning and stopped to take a leak before heading upstairs. There was a bathroom around the corner from the office that no one ever used, a small bathroom with a single urinal and stall. I don't know what possessed me, but I've always liked to mess around in bathrooms. Old habits die hard. I walked in and the stall door stared back at me with a funny look on its face.

"Hi-ya!" I yelled, running and throwing a roundhouse karate kick at my target. I didn't actually know martial arts, but I'd seen the move on TV. The door banged open and slammed shut after ricocheting off the wall.

"Ahh!" someone screamed.

Huh! I didn't expect anybody to be in there. Like I said, no one ever uses this bathroom.

"Peter, I'm gonna kill you!" Jeffrey barged out of the stall. I had scared the snot out of him, all right—I could tell. He must have sprayed everywhere. He had wet spots all over his pants. I wanted to laugh, but Jeffrey glared at me.

I backed to the door. "I—I didn't know you were in there. I swear."

"You better grow eyes in the back of your head," he warned.

I yanked the door open and hurried upstairs while Jeffrey stayed behind, probably to dry his pants. I got to work helping Mr. T.

If you've ever moved, then you know it's all about boxes. Packing boxes, lifting boxes, and unpacking boxes. Boxes, boxes, and more boxes. After a while I got sick of them, so I tried cramming one with as much as I could fit, thinking that more stuff in each box would mean less boxes all together in the end. Luke, our class brainiac, would have been proud of my smarts. The problem was, I forgot about needing to lift the box after jamming it full of books and anything else I could get inside.

"Peter, you've got too much in there," Anna warned. "You should take some stuff out."

I liked Anna and all, but I wasn't about to listen to a girl. I managed to pick the box up after almost getting a hernia, but then the stupid bottom fell out. I stood there like a dork, holding an empty cardboard box with junk all around my feet. Mr. T and Ms. Newberry got a good chuckle, and I know Anna had to bite her tongue.

After the super-heavy box strategy failed, I decided I'd take two normal-sized boxes and stack them one on top of the other. My idea was that two at once would lead to fewer box trips. Luke would have been proud again. The problem this time wasn't that they were too heavy, but that I couldn't *see* very well. I got the two lifted and started on my way, but I didn't make it very far before I ran into one of the classroom desks. The corner hit me right in the you-know-what. I dropped the boxes and balled up on the ground, groaning and holding my privates. You'd think a boy would get some sympathy from a male teacher after an injury like that, but Mr. T had a funny way of showing he cared.

"Ahh, c'mon. You're all right, Peter," he said. "They're just peanuts."

Even with my injury, he made me smile. Of course everyone else thought it was hysterical, especially Lexie.

"Ohh, poor Peter's peanuts," she sang. "Hey, it's a tongue twister. Poor Peter's Peanuts. Poor Peter's—"

"Okay, Lexie," Mr. T said.

She thought it was a riot. She couldn't stop laughing. And then she got to laughing so hard that she farted—right out loud! A real stinker! Served her right. Lexie turned bright red in the face. I wasn't about to let her off easy by pretending nothing had happened.

"Oh my God!" I yelled.

"What now?" Mr. T asked, looking up from the box he had gone back to packing.

"Peter farted," Lexie was quick to say.

"What! No way! That was you!" I was ready to wring her neck.

"That's classic cover-up, Peter," she said. "Blaming someone else."

"Are you nuts?!"

"We *know* you hurt your peanuts," she said. "We're sorry."

"That's enough, you two," Mr. T said. "Someone farted. I don't care who, just don't do it again. It stinks." He covered his nose with his shirt and so did a laughing Ms. Newberry.

Lexie flashed me her devil smile.

"Better go check your underwear after that one," I whispered. The only good thing about her fart was that it somehow made me forget about my privates hurting.

And so went my summer: watch out for Jeffrey, deal with Lexie, and hang with Mr. T. I had a good time.

Alexia

Summer was pretty cool. The only bad part was that Mom was still waiting tables from noon to close every day, so she spent most mornings sleeping. So like, I was pretty much on my own. But no biggie—it'd been that way for a while now.

In the beginning, I rode my bike over to the school a lot and helped Teach with the classroom move. I liked doing that. Hanging with Teach was cool after spending all that time without him. I wasn't the only one around. Jessica was gone to some writing thing and Luke was away, but Anna and Jeffrey were in the classroom a lot, and Danielle was busy on her farm but still came by often. Ms. Newberry was there every day, smiling and making Teach smile, and of course, there was also Peter. I loved teasing Peter. He'd try to give it back, but I always won. He was a good sport about it, though. It was all fun, not like mean-girl stuff. And I would know. So for a while, that was what I did with my summer. I'd never complain about time spent with Teach. Not after what we all went through.

But then one day, when I was riding home from school, I heard some voices coming from the abandoned house on Old Woods Road. I rode past this house every day. I'd been in it before. It could be a pretty cool hangout spot, but it was kinda scary, too. Dust and cobwebs, cracked window glass, a creaky floor, falling-down boards, and rusty nails—the place was old. Real old, and probably not very safe. But like, I wanted to see who was in it.

After leaving my bike on the grass, I crossed the porch and crept into the front of the house where there was a doorway, but no door. I tried to walk softly as I snooped around, but the boards made noise under my feet. I didn't hear them coming from behind me.

"Who're you?"

"Ahh!" I screamed, scared out of my mind. I spun around fast and saw two faces.

"Sorry," the first girl said.

"What're you doin' here, Little Brat?" the second girl said.

They were older. High school girls, I could tell. They were bigger than me for one, and like, they needed bras where I still had my flat chest.

"Stop, Reena," the first girl said. "You're gonna scare her."

"I'm just jokin'. Gimme a break." Reena looked at me. "Don't worry. You can chill here, Little Brat." She turned and walked away. "I'll be in the back," she called over her shoulder.

"I'm Lisa," the first girl said. "What's your name?"

"Alexia, but my friends call me Lexie."

"C'mon, Lexie." She put her arm around me and gave me a tour of their hangout. The place wasn't dirty and creepy anymore. They'd cleaned it up, the back room especially. They had put some old carpet pieces on the floor, which were a lot better than the creaky boards with rusty nails. There was a green couch and a brown armchair, and then some lawn furniture. In the middle of the room they had plywood laid across cinder blocks for a table. And they had a few blankets tacked over the windows for a little privacy—or secrecy.

Lisa was very pretty. She had dark hair with tight curls cropped close to her head. It looked good, especially with her dark maroon lipstick. She had a nice body that she showed off in short shorts and a tank top.

"Grab a seat, Lexie. You can chill with us," Lisa said.

I accepted her invite, not wanting to be rude and not wanting to make them mad. I sat down in the brown armchair. Reena was already sitting on the couch, and something told me not to sit next to her. I stared at the floor because I wasn't sure what else to do.

"Hey, you're back," Lisa said.

I looked up and saw her walk over to kiss the sweaty boy who'd just arrived.

"Who's this?" he said, nodding at me.

"Alexia," Lisa said, "but her friends call her Lexie."

"Hey, Alexia," the boy said. "I'm Brandon." He nodded toward the couch. "And that's Reena over there."

"They've already met," Lisa said.

"Brandon's a big bad football player and wrestler," Reena teased.

He made a face at her. "That's right," he said. "I am. I just got done with a run." He looked at me now. "I'm starting my training."

"Oh," I said. He sure seemed big and bad.

When I looked over at Reena she had her lips curled around a cigarette. She was as pretty as Lisa, but she made me nervous.

"Hey, Lexie. Want one?" Reena said, holding out another cigarette. "Or are you a little Goody Two-shoes?"

Jessica

FADE IN: LONG SHOT (LS) of JESSICA sitting in a classroom with a bunch of other kids. Kids we've never seen before, some older, some the same age. It's obvious this is a classroom devoted to writing. There are books all along the walls, plenty of computers, and an assortment of papers, pencils, pens, and highlighters. All the students are working. Some of them are drafting, others editing, and one is conferencing with the instructor.

JESSICA VOICE-OVER (VO)

I spent the bulk of my summer in New York City at Columbia University, participating in a writing camp. A couple of times a week Mom would ride the train into the city from New Haven. She'd work on her own writing while I was at camp, then we'd spend time together in the afternoon and evening. The camp was amazing. I had to submit a piece when I applied, and based on that I was accepted. I wrote about Mr. Terupt. That was easy. He's the best man in the world. I was fortunate I'd be having him as my teacher again, and to have been selected for the writing program. My favorite part of the camp was our unit spent on screenwriting.

FADE OUT.

anna

For me, a few things stood out from the summer. My mom still worked a few days a week at her school, doing library stuff and helping with the summer programs, but I got to spend a lot of time with her. Mom was also spending time with Charlie, and she was very happy. It made me feel good. I liked Charlie too. Mom also kept busy with her artwork. She entered one of her pieces in a show in New York City. We got to go down there for a few days, which was a lot of fun. I even visited with Jessica. She was in some sort of writing camp taking place at Columbia University. The four of us, our moms and me and Jessica, had lunch in some fancy little café.

I also saw Danielle over the summer. Mom and I would go to the farm and visit—Charlie didn't just come to our house. Danielle's mom and dad were more accepting of me and Mom now, so it wasn't that big a deal for us to go over to their place. Her grandma and grandpa still never spoke to us, however. But the farm was great! My favorite part was helping Charlie and Danielle with the nighttime milking. My first time doing it, Charlie said, "Anna, come take a look at this." He was sitting beside one of the cows, getting ready to put the machine on her. When I bent closer to look, he squeezed her teat and milk shot into my face.

"You just fell for the oldest trick in the book," Danielle said, laughing.

The other thing I did over the summer was help Mr. Terupt move our classroom down to the sixth-grade annex. I did this on those days Mom had to work, though Mom even came to help a few times. Peter helped too, or tried to. Somehow his good intentions often turned into mess-ups, but I had fun with him. Most of the time I was laughing. Like the day he crammed all he could into one box. I tried to warn him, but he didn't want to listen. When it was time to lift the box, Peter grunted and groaned. He turned all red in the face just getting it off the ground. As soon as he stood up, the bottom of the box fell out. Stuff crashed to the floor and scattered everywhere. I tried not to laugh, but that was hard.

Then Peter tried carrying more than one box, but he hurt himself (in the bad spot) because he couldn't see where he was going. As if that wasn't bad enough, the next thing he did was let loose a terrible-smelling fart. Then he tried to blame Lexie for it. Imagine her farting—please!

Next he decided he was going to carry a tower of books

to our new room. He said he'd had enough of boxes, and figured he could carry more as a tower anyway. Those chapter books can have slippery covers. I tried telling him, but no.

"Peter, they're not LEGOs," I said.

"Ta-da!" He stood up with his tower, his bottom hand by his knees, his top hand above his eyes. He took a few steps and then it happened. The middle book sprang free, setting off a domino effect of books shooting out of his tower like bullets. After the frenzy, Peter stood there with one book in his hands.

"Maybe you should try a different approach," Mr. Terupt said, chuckling—again.

"I wanted to see if it would work," Peter said.

"Well, now you know," Mr. Terupt said. "But that's good. You were experimenting. That's science. I like that."

Peter looked at me and shrugged. I smiled and shook my head.

Despite his mess-ups, Peter showed up every day to help. As long as his mess-ups didn't turn into an accident like last year, I was fine with his good intentions.

The annex was a little complex separate from the main school building. It looked just like the main school, same red brick and windows, but it wasn't attached.

"Mr. Terupt, why do we even have an annex?" I asked. We were carrying boxes down to our new room. "I've never seen another school with one."

"Well, my best guess is that at some point, the town must have decided they needed more space for all the students, so the annex was constructed. It was probably the wisest solution."

The annex wasn't far from the main building, just a short distance down the sidewalk out the side door, but it was still a lot of work to move. We had to box up all of Mr. Terupt's things, move them, and then unpack them and get the stuff put away. That's the part I liked, the putting-away part. I liked it because then I got to decide how to arrange our new classroom, and I liked it because I got to do it with Ms. Newberry. She was also there every day.

There were some beautiful bookcases in our new room. A few low-to-the-ground ones and a couple that climbed up the side wall. Mr. Terupt had plenty of books for the shelves. He had old ones and new ones. One day I opened an older-looking one, *Belle Prater's Boy* by Ruth White, and I saw an inscription: *Happy Twelfth Birthday, William. Love, Mom.* Below it, Mr. Terupt had written his full name, *William Owen Terupt*, and his home address. His books were his treasures, just like they were for Jessica.

William was a good name for Mr. Terupt. He could be serious and taken seriously like a William, he could be fun and a bit wild and crazy like a young boy named Billy, or maybe he was a young handsome catch named Will. Mr. Terupt had a great personality. William was the perfect name for him.

I read his book—*Belle Prater's Boy*. I had gotten into reading more because of Mr. Terupt and Jessica. The story was about a boy missing his mama, wondering what happened to her. It made me wonder more about my father and who he was.

I spent several days working with Ms. Newberry, organizing Mr. Terupt's books on those shelves.

"You like him, don't you?" I said, working next to her one day. I couldn't hold it in any longer. I had to ask so I could hear her answer.

"Of course I like him, Anna. Everyone likes Mr. Terupt."

"No," I said. "Not like that. I mean, you really like him, don't you?"

Now she stopped. She looked down at the books in her hands and smiled. Then she looked at me, still smiling. But before she answered, Ms. Newberry asked me a question.

"What makes you think that, Anna? Is it because I'm here every day?"

"No," I said. "It's not that. It's the way you look at him."

"Oh," she said. And then her smile grew even bigger.

When we finished we had a great reading corner with lots of light from the windows on our back wall. I knew Jessica was going to like that. There was also a row of cabinets with a nice countertop all along the window area and a back door that was all glass and that opened directly to the outside. Our front door opened to the hallway inside the annex. We had a sink area on the wall opposite the books, and next to the sink stood several tall cabinets for storage. We arranged the desks in tables of four. I liked our new room, and so did Mr. Terupt. When he first looked at our finished reading corner, he was all smiles.

I didn't tell Ms. Newberry, but it wasn't just the way she looked at him. It was the way he looked at her, too.

Jeffrey

The school year ended with good news. Real good news. But that was where it stopped. There was still hardly anything between Mom and Dad, and I didn't know how to fix it. Dad would leave for work every morning and Mom would stay home. She got dressed most days, but not all. Sometimes she made dinner, but not often, and when she did, we ate separately, never as a family.

Dad was a self-employed handyman, so he didn't have to work with people, and he worked when he wanted and as much as he wanted. Mom had a job at Home Depot in one of the managerial positions before my brother, Michael, died. That's how she and Dad met. He was in the store getting materials when he first saw her. He liked what he saw, so he kept finding reasons to go back. He would ask for her help every time, and one thing led to another. But now they barely talk. And Mom isn't ready to deal with lots of people the way she had to at work. So she stays home.

I chose to go to school every chance I got. I helped Terupt move our classroom. Peter, Anna, Alexia, and Danielle helped, too. Was it because their homes stunk, like mine? Or was it because they wanted to be there? I could tell Ms. Newberry wanted to be there. I wished Mom and Dad felt for each other the way it seemed Terupt and Ms. Newberry did. How do you get that back once it's gone? I wondered.

I missed Jessica and Luke not bein' around. I was ready for school to start. What a difference a year with Terupt made.

LUKE

I spent my summer at science camp. It was something my mom had signed me up for before Mr. Terupt's accident, and she insisted that I attend because it would be good for me to get away for a little while. She knew I'd try to spend every day at school with Mr. Terupt, otherwise.

"He wants you to go, honey," Mom said. "You can see him when you get back."

The camp was awesome! It was at the Science Minds Museum. We were given materials and challenged to invent different things. We studied all sorts of critters and habitats. We conducted experiments and worked with chemicals. I didn't tell anyone, but I figured out where I went wrong with my plant concoction that caused it to go bonkers and set off the fire alarm last year. My favorite part of the camp was our work as detectives, though. We were given a Mystery of the

Day and then challenged to work with our team to uncover clues and ultimately solve the mystery.

When the camp ended I visited Mr. Terupt. Our classroom had been moved down to the annex, so that's where I found him, and Jeffrey. The room looked terrific. "Peter, Anna, and Jeffrey helped out a lot," Mr. Terupt said. "Alexia was here quite a bit too in the beginning of the summer, but not so much lately."

"I brought you a gift," I said. I went out into the hall and grabbed my surprise. "One of the things I loved at science camp was the tank habitats of various animals located throughout the museum, so I put one together for our classroom. I have two anoles in here, Jackson and Lincoln, named after two of our presidents, number seven, Andrew Jackson, and number sixteen, Abraham Lincoln. I did some reading this summer about the presidents on our currency. Jackson's on the twenty-dollar bill and Lincoln's on the penny and the five-dollar bill."

"Wow!" Jeffrey said. "That's awesome!"

"The tank looks beautiful, Luke," Mr. Terupt said. "Thank you."

"Can we put it on the back counter?" Jeffrey asked. "That's the perfect place for it." Jeffrey carried the tank away before Mr. Terupt could even answer.

"Tell me, Luke, what exactly are anoles?" Mr. Terupt asked.

"They're often called chameleons because of their color-changing ability, though they look nothing alike and chameleons come from different parts of the world," I said. "The color changing is a camouflage technique, but if they turn dark brown for too long, that's a sign of them being stressed or sick. It's really important not to let them get dehydrated. We need to wet the bog two or three times a day with this spray bottle."

"Whoa! That guy just grabbed a cricket and bit his head off!" Jeffrey yelled. Mr. Terupt and I smiled at each other.

I walked over and gave Jeffrey the spray bottle and showed him what to do; then I told Mr. Terupt all about my science camp.

"We'll see if all that work helps you solve this year's riddles," he said.

One thing I learned at camp was that scientists don't start with the answers, and sometimes they never even find the answers. Instead, they are almost always asking questions. Questions that come from their observations. And they can only make these observations if they pay attention to everything and use all their senses. So I planned to pay attention and ask lots of questions in sixth grade.

QUESTIONS
—Why isn't Lexie around as much now?
—What riddles?

Detective Luke

Alexia

"You ever smoke before, Goody Two-shoes?" Reena asked me.

"Yeah," I lied. I didn't like her calling me that. That was what I used to call Jessica—when I was being mean.

"Yeah, right," she said. "What're you, in kindergarten?"

"Sixth," I said.

"It's all right if you haven't before. You're young," Lisa said. "You probably haven't had the chance."

"Sixth grade is a good time to try it," Reena said. She put a cigarette in her mouth and lit it. Then she passed it to Lisa, who handed it to me.

"It's no sweat, Lexie. You'll see next year—everybody does it," Lisa said.

"It helps you take the edge off, Little Brat. Give it a try. You'll see."

"I'd join ya, but I can't," Brandon said. "It's training season."

I didn't know what else to do, so I brought the white stick to my mouth. I curled my lips around it and sucked in. Instantly, I started coughing my head off. It tasted awful, and it made my lungs burn like there was a fire in my chest!

"That's it." Brandon slapped me on the back. "You'll get the hang of it."

"Do you have a boyfriend, Lexie?" Lisa asked me.

I noticed the dark maroon circle smudged around her cigarette from her lipstick. Reena's circle was fire-engine red. "No," I said, and hacked some more.

"The boys should be hot after you," Reena said. "You're a pretty little brat."

I was wearing pink shorts with a white T-shirt and flip-flops. My hair was pulled back with a fancy heart scrunchie.

"It's time you ditch that baby lip gloss and try some real lipstick," Reena said. "And lose the scrunchie."

I shrugged. I was okay with that.

Lisa gave me an elastic to use in my hair and she helped me wipe off my Princess Pink lip gloss and apply her dark maroon lipstick. "You can keep that," she said, giving me the tube.

"Thanks," I said.

I looked at the dark maroon circle around my cigarette in between coughs.

"Now, that's fresh," Brandon said about my new look.

"Totally," Lisa agreed.

Suddenly my cheeks and ears burned like my chest. I

couldn't look at Brandon. I liked getting complimented by a boy, even though I knew this one was taken.

After I finished my cigarette, Reena decided it was time for me to leave. "It's gonna be gettin' past your bedtime. I think you should probably go." She led me back to the front.

When we got to the porch, Reena grabbed me by my elbow. "Listen, Little Brat. You can come back and chill with us anytime. You don't need to be scared, but you better not tell anybody about our hangout, or else." She squeezed my arm hard and smiled at the same time.

I left.

Danielle

My summer was great! A lot of kids complain that they get bored over the summer, but not me. I got to do a bunch of different things. Some days I spent at school helping Mr. Terupt; other days I spent on the farm. Either I pitched in with Grandma and Mom, learning more as I helped them cook and sew, or I gave Charlie a hand with the milking and walking the pastures, checking on the cows getting ready to calf. I also rode the tractors with Dad and Grandpa, and helped them fix whatever needed fixing. And Grandma and I tended to the garden together. That was an everyday thing.

There were also times when Anna came over with her mother. Anna and I found all sorts of things to do together, and once in a while Anna hung out with my brother and I hung out with her mom. That's when I got to do some art-work with Terri, but we always did it out of sight of Grandma and Grandpa. Mom and Dad had grown comfortable around Terri. Mom even offered Terri coffee or pie when she came over, and she was getting better at having conversation with her.

Every day was different in a good way. In fact, I can only remember two bad days. One was on the hottest afternoon of the season when a group of us decided to go to the public pool. I had just put my stuff down when some jerk walked by and said, "No whales allowed." No one else heard him, but I didn't even get in the water. That was definitely a crummy day, but this other time upset me more because I didn't understand why what happened was a big deal.

I was outside. It was sunny, both hot and bright, and I was sweating. I was with Grandma, working in the garden. I wasn't right next to her, so it wasn't until I looked up that I saw she was over with Grandpa, peering off into the distance. I shaded my eyes and looked as hard as I could. The only thing I could make out was a man walking across our fields. He was way far out, so I couldn't tell much about him. But I could tell that Grandma and Grandpa were getting all mad. They made hard arm gestures and Grandpa stomped away. When Grandma turned toward me, I saw her twisted and pained face.

I walked over to where she stood. "Grandma, what's wrong?"

"Nothin'."

"Grandma, I saw that man walking across our fields and I saw you and Grandpa. What's wrong?"

"I said nothin'. Now back to pickin' those weeds and don't ask me any more questions."

Later that night, I found my family sitting around the kitchen table in serious discussion. When I walked in, the talking stopped. I knew something was up, and it wasn't "nothin'," like Grandma had said.

That's the day that kept coming back to me. I didn't know what it was all about, but I had a feeling it wasn't good. I kept staring out into our fields, and so did Grandpa, but I never spotted anyone else out there.

Dear God,

I'm not sure what that man was doing in our fields. I'm not sure who he was. But he seems to have given Grandpa, and the rest of my family, a lot to worry about. Please comfort them, and help me figure out what's going on. And God, this isn't as important, especially 'cause I know how busy you must be, but if you do have the time, I'd like it if you could teach that mean boy from the pool a lesson. Thanks. Amen.

september

Jessica

FADE IN: Camera starts with an aerial view of Snow Hill School. We see children entering the building with brand-new backpacks and bright sneakers. Camera follows JESSICA as she walks through the front entrance. We see teachers greeting students as they arrive. We follow JESSICA out the side door and down to the annex, where we find MR. TERUPT standing outside his door.

JESSICA VO
(while approaching Mr. Terupt)

The start of another school year with Mr. Terupt is upon us. I'm thinking about happy endings. Mr. Terupt and I both like them. I'm hoping for another one this year.

MR. TERUPT

Hello, Miss Jessica. You look very nice.

JESSICA
(with a slight bow)
Thank you. You look handsome yourself.

A proud MR. TERUPT smooths his tie and tips his head in appreciation.

JESSICA
I'm really excited to do this all again.

MR. TERUPT
(leaning closer to Jessica)
Me too. Let's be sure to finish with another happy ending.

JESSICA
(walking into the classroom)
You can count on me.

JESSICA VO
Roller-coaster rides have always been my favorite. After all the ups and downs and twists and turns, I always get off them laughing and smiling. Fifth grade was a bit of a roller coaster, but it was one that I don't need to go on again. I'm hoping for more of a merry-go-round with sixth grade.

FADE OUT.

Peter

Imagine being reminded of the worst thing you ever did—every single day for the rest of your whole entire life. I suppose people sentenced to life in prison might feel that way. I still thought about that day in the snow all the time, especially when I was with Mr. T.

You know how when you see something different or unusual, it's hard not to stare? But after a while, you get used to it and then you don't need to keep staring? Mr. T had a dent on the side of his head where they did the surgery. I used to stare at it all the time on those days when I was helping him, but eventually I got used to it. Getting used to it didn't mean it stopped reminding me of that snowball, though. I wasn't ever forgetting about that.

In some ways the start of school was no different from the summer. Richard went back to his prep school, Northfield

Mount Hermon, and Mom and Dad kept up business as usual. That left just me and Miss Catalina, our au pair, at home.

The different part was that the clock started ticking. I knew it was going to be an awesome sixth-grade year with Mr. T manning the controls, but I also knew this was the beginning of the end. There was no chance of Mr. T following us to seventh grade, because there was no seventh grade at Snow Hill School. Instead, we'd have sixth-grade graduation, then move on to the regional high school. That was true for everyone but me. My new school would be Riverway, an all-boys' junior boarding school for grades seven and eight located in Massachusetts. The same school my brother, father, grandfather, and great-grandfather had all attended. So this was it. . . .

Until I came up with one of my brilliant ideas. An idea so smart Luke would have been proud. My plan was to fail—on purpose! I'd fail sixth grade, then I'd have to repeat the year with Mr. T. It was ingenious.

I never dreamed of wanting to do that before. Make school last longer, that is. It wasn't about school, though, just my time with Mr. T. And that's the other thing. Since my time with Mr. T was so special to me, the days flew by.

LUKE

It had to be on all our minds. Would this year be like last year? Before the snowball? Last year Mr. Terupt had one awesome idea after another. Would it be like that again? I got my answer right away.

"Okay, gang. There's no point in waiting, so let's get started," Mr. Terupt announced. "I have our first book here, and with it . . . there will be a competition."

I sat up straight. I looked at Jessica, and we both smiled. Yes! I thought.

"The book we're going to use is *The Westing Game* by Ellen Raskin." Mr. Terupt held the book up for us to see. "It won the Newbery Medal in 1979."

"Oooh, Newberry," Peter teased. "Like a real pretty teacher here."

"There's no connection between the medal and Ms.

Newberry—thank you, Peter," Mr. Terupt said. "Though she is just as special," he added under his breath.

It was good to see Peter teasing Mr. Terupt. I hoped Peter could get back some of his fun self. Just not too much of it.

"What's it about?" Marty asked.

"What's the competition?" I asked.

"Slow down, fellas," Mr. Terupt said. "I'm getting there. Give me a second." Mr. Terupt took a deep breath and paused for a moment while holding on to the front table, his eyes closed. Then he continued. "This story is a murder mystery. The competition is a race to see who can solve the crime first."

Yes! I thought again.

"As soon as you think you know, you will write down your guess along with an explanation of how you got your answer. You'll put your solution in a sealed envelope and it will stay sealed until we finish the book. We'll finish the last few chapters together in class, and then we'll open each of your solutions to see who got it right, or who came the closest. We'll make it a special ceremony."

"This is going to be awesome!" I exclaimed.

"Calm down, Luke. Let Mr. Terupt finish," Wendy said.

Mr. Terupt nodded. "As soon as you think you have it figured out, you can submit your solution. If two people get it right, then the person who submitted first wins. So don't forget to date your solutions."

Here was our first riddle. Awesome! After my summer science training, there was no way I was going to miss out on solving this mystery.

"Lastly," Mr. Terupt continued, "since I've never read the book, I will also take part in this competition." He looked right at me after saying that.

"You're going down," Peter said to Mr. Terupt. It was nice having Peter on my side.

Mr. Terupt chuckled. The challenge was on.

QUESTION
—How special does Mr. Terupt think Ms. Newberry really is?

Detective Luke

ANNA

Mr. Terupt sent his book team (that's what he called me and Peter after all the book moving we did this summer) to the library to get copies of *The Westing Game*. Lexie and Luke came with us because they had arrived early that morning as well. Mr. Terupt didn't need to send all four of us, but the errand gave us something to do. The plan was to start *The Westing Game* later that day, but that didn't actually happen because, well, something else did.

We stopped in the office on our way back from the library to pick up Mr. Terupt's mail as a favor to him. That's when Luke made one of his famous observations. Ever since his summer science camp he was determined to notice everything—"like a detective," he would say. I don't think his brain ever stops working.

"Where's Mrs. Williams?" Luke asked. "She's always here for the morning announcements."

"Maybe she's in the bathroom," Lexie said.

"Doing what? Powdering her nose?" Peter wisecracked.

Those two never stopped going back and forth. They reminded me of that old cartoon with the coyote and road-runner. The roadrunner always outwitted the coyote, but the coyote never learned. Lexie was the roadrunner. After Peter made his wisecrack, she reached over when he wasn't looking and knocked all the books out of his hands.

"Hey, you jerk!" Peter yelled. "You're gonna get it."

"Whatever," Lexie said. She walked out of the office with a smirk and an extra shake in her hips. In my head I heard her saying, "Beep-beep." Like the roadrunner, she'd won again.

I helped Peter pick up his books; then we left the office behind Lexie and Luke. I did wonder where Mrs. Williams was, but Lexie's answer made sense. I decided not to worry about it, but that changed once we got to the doors heading down to the annex. Just as we pushed them open, Ms. New-berry came rushing through in the opposite direction. She was crying. And she didn't stop to talk.

"Must be her time of the month, all emotional and sensi-tive like that," Lexie said.

"Must be your time of the month to be stupid," Peter said. "Wait, that's every day for you."

I didn't even know what they were talking about, "time of the month," and I didn't get a chance to ask, nor did Lexie get a chance to come back at Peter, because Luke made an-other one of his observations. And this was a big one.

"Look!" He pointed.

An ambulance and a police car were parked next to

the annex. Peter's books fell all over the ground (this time without anyone's help) as he took off sprinting toward our classroom.

When Mr. Terupt collapsed after being hit by Peter's snowball, I was scared. Scared like I'd never been before. I didn't know what to do. I sank to my knees in horror. My hands covered my mouth and tears ran down my cheeks. I hoped I'd never feel like that again, certainly not so soon. But the sight of that ambulance, Ms. Newberry rushing by us crying, and Peter running to our classroom, all took me back to that day in the snow.

Jeffrey

It's hard to believe what happened—but it did. I swear it on my brother Michael's grave.

I was riding my bike to school, same as always. I liked riding my bike because then I wasn't stuck in the car with Mom or Dad with nothing to talk about. And I hated taking the bus even more because all that stop-and-go always makes me sick. So I was riding my bike, and I was almost there. I was just around the bend, where there's a field on one side and woods on the other, when I heard it. It's lucky that I did hear it. It was a faint crying sound.

I looked over in the direction of the sound and spotted a black duffel bag with something beside it in the weeds. It wasn't far off the road. I dumped my bike and walked over. I figured it was a kitten. But as I got closer I knew it was something else. First I saw the blue blanket, and then I saw what was tucked inside a shoe box.

It was a baby! A real live baby! On the side of the road in a shoe box! I was scared. Real scared. I didn't know what to do. I tried helpin' him as best I could.

He was a mess, and so was the blanket. I had no idea how long he'd been there, but he had peed and pooped all over and he felt very cold. I took my sweatshirt off and spread it on the ground. Then I lifted him out of the box and he started wailing. I wrapped him up in my shirt, grabbed the duffel bag, and picked him up.

"You're gonna be all right, little buddy. I gotcha."

I left my bike and walked the rest of the way to school, cradling the baby. He calmed down some, and so did I. But once I got to school, I got really nervous and scared again. I rushed to Terupt. The nice thing about being in the annex was we didn't have to go through the whole school to get to our classroom. You could get there just by walking up to it from outside.

As soon as Terupt heard the crying, he looked up.

"I found him on the side of the road!" I said.

Jessica

FADE IN: LS of the classroom. We see JESSICA and DAN-
IELLE sitting in the book area, with two classmates. Others
sit at their desks and a few are still trickling into the classroom from the hall. MS. NEWBERRY is visiting with MR.
TERUPT, like she does most mornings before the start of the
school day.

CUT TO: JEFFREY rushing through the back door with a
crying baby in his arms and a black duffel bag slung over his
shoulder.

JEFFREY
I found him on the side of the road!

JESSICA VO
It wasn't going to be a merry-go-round year. We were on another roller coaster that took off the moment Jeffrey walked

in with that poor baby. The best roller coasters always include lots of screaming and yelling. That's part of the fun, but I wasn't screaming and yelling with excitement this time. I was holding on to Danielle.

PULL BACK: MS. NEWBERRY hurries to the classroom phone and calls 911. MR. TERUPT rushes over to JEFFREY and takes the baby. He kneels and gently places the crying infant down on the floor.

MR. TERUPT

Jeffrey, what's in the duffel bag?

JESSICA VO

Jeffrey stood blank-faced, staring down at Mr. Terupt and the baby. Shock was clearly setting in. He probably hadn't had time to think about the situation when he was busy caring for the baby, but once he handed him over to Mr. Terupt, I saw Jeffrey's body go weak.

MR. TERUPT
(forcefully)

Jeffrey!

JEFFREY
(snapping out of his trance)

What? Oh, I don't know.

JEFFREY bends down and opens the zipper of the duffel bag. He pulls out a diaper and wipes.

MR. TERUPT

Perfect. Let me have them.

JEFFREY hands the diaper and wipes to MR. TERUPT.

MR. TERUPT
(under his breath)

At least they left him with something.

JESSICA VO

I don't like saying this, but when Mr. Terupt undid that little baby's dirty diaper, it reeked worse than Danielle's barn. I had to turn my head away to keep from gagging.

CUT TO: MRS. WILLIAMS enters the classroom—unprepared.

MRS. WILLIAMS

Oh my goodness!

Her hands fly up and cover her mouth. MS. NEWBERRY walks over and hugs her. The two women are both teary-eyed.

JESSICA VO

I understood why they were crying. This baby had been left on the side of the road. Where were his parents? I thought about Anna. How would she react to all this? I felt Danielle squeeze me, and that gave me some hope. I knew her prayers were with that baby.

CUT TO: An ambulance and police car pull up to the classroom. The paramedics and police officer hurry inside and take

over for **MR. TERUPT** and **JEFFREY. MR. TERUPT** stands and puts his arm around **JEFFREY** and pulls him close. **MS. NEWBERRY** walks over and leans into **MR. TERUPT.** She puts her head on his shoulder and he wraps his other arm around her.

> MR. TERUPT
> (to both of them)
> Don't worry. Everything will be okay.

> JESSICA VO
> Would it? Mr. Terupt was playing the role of the comforter, trying to make everyone feel better. I wonder, would he have told us the same thing last year, when he was lying in a coma? Would he have said to us then, "Don't worry, everything will be okay"? He would have been right. I hope he's right this time.

Paramedics tend to the crying baby. They check him all over with various instruments, and then hook up an IV.

> MS. NEWBERRY
> (to Mr. Terupt)
> I need to go to my classroom. My students will be wondering where I am.

> MR. TERUPT
> I know. Go on. It's okay. I'll see you after school.

MS. NEWBERRY leaves, her eyes welling with fresh tears.

JESSICA VO

That wouldn't be the only time I saw Ms. Newberry with tears in her eyes this year.

CUT TO: PETER running into the classroom and stopping. LUKE, LEXIE, and ANNA burst in right after him. They all look paralyzed. They are statues, unable to move or speak.

CUT TO: A paramedic lifts the baby off the ground and carries him to the ambulance. A second paramedic walks beside them holding a bag of fluid that is attached to the baby. We see the ambulance doors close. We watch it drive away.

CUT TO: LS of the classroom. No one has moved. It remains silent. Camera zooms in on LUKE.

LUKE

Mr. Terupt, where are the baby's parents?

FADE OUT.

LUKE

I barged into the classroom just in time. The paramedics were bent over some small, softly wailing bundle. My ears told me what it was, but I took a few sideways steps so that I could see it to believe it. Sure enough, it was a baby. The baby was sucking intermittently on a wet washcloth, which explained the muffled cries. I also saw that an IV had been started. I knew from my previous science studies and Boy Scouts that the baby was suffering from dehydration. What my experience and background knowledge hadn't prepared me for was the answer Mr. Terupt gave my question after the ambulance sped away.

"Mr. Terupt, where are the baby's parents?" I asked.

"It appears he was abandoned, Luke," Mr. Terupt said. "His mom and dad didn't want him, so he was left on the side of the road. Jeffrey found him this morning."

Our classroom was still and full of nerves when I walked in. I didn't think there was room for any other feelings, but after Mr. Terupt said that, a shocked sadness consumed us. The air I breathed felt heavier. How could anyone do that to their baby?

That was when the police officer in attendance told Jeffrey he needed to talk to him since he had discovered the baby. It made me realize this was a case for a detective, and that everyone had made a huge blunder. Important evidence had been ruined when they cleaned up the baby.

QUESTIONS
—Who and where are the baby's parents?
—Will we ever know?

Detective Luke

Jeffrey

Officer Stoneley was a big man—built like a block—with buzzed hair, sideburns, and a goatee. He wasn't a donut policeman—one of those guys with a huge belly that rubbed on his steering wheel. He looked strong.

Stoneley took my report. Basically, I just had to tell him what happened. Afterward, we took a ride in his car over to the spot where I had found the baby. He needed to see the area and he wanted me to walk him through the details again.

There were several other police cars already on the scene when Stoneley and I got there. I wasn't expecting that, or the yellow tape that had the area marked off. This was a real investigation. A woman was taking pictures and another man and woman were inspecting the shoe box and blanket. I showed those to Stoneley. Everything was still there.

Officer Stoneley didn't say anything, but his stone face turned soft. I could see that even behind his dark sunglasses. His body language told how terrible he felt. He grimaced and shook his head. And his shoulders slumped as he let out a sigh.

We stood there side by side for a minute, not saying anything. That was when I started thinking about Michael. Mom and Dad did everything in their power to save my brother. And today I had found a baby that somebody just threw away. How could anyone do that?

"All right," Stoneley said. "That's it. Let's go."

We threw my bike in the trunk of his car and he gave me a ride back to school.

"Okay, Jeffrey," Stoneley said as we pulled up to the front doors, "we're all set."

"Will you find his parents?" I asked, still staring out the front windshield like Stoneley.

"Hard to say," he answered. "We'll try." Then there was another one of those silent moments before he took off his sunglasses and looked at me. "You did good today, kid."

That was nice of him to say, but it didn't feel like it.

Peter

Mrs. Williams walked over to Mr. T and asked him if he was okay. He told her he'd let her know if he needed anything.

"What about them?" she asked, meaning us. She looked at our class with a worried face. We weren't just any kids to her, and you could tell she really felt bad.

"We're fine, Mrs. Williams," Lexie said.

Mrs. Williams smiled and nodded.

"I'll talk to them," Mr. T told her.

"I'll put a letter together," she said.

He nodded. The letter was for us to take home to our parents, so they could be made aware of the crazy day we'd had. It wasn't the first letter with shocking news to come from our classroom. My parents probably wouldn't have time for this one either.

"Let's talk, gang," Mr. T said, once it was just us in the classroom. He sat on his desk. "I'm sorry I was so gruff when I answered your question, Luke. I shouldn't have said that."

"But it's the truth," Luke said. "We can handle the truth."

Mr. T sighed. "Yes, unfortunately, I think what I said probably is the truth. But let's keep in mind we don't know the whole story." He stood and walked closer to us. "This is a situation that most adults would prefer to keep from children, because it's not something you need to know or worry about at your age. But there was no protecting you from it today. The world can be a harsh place and you witnessed that cold reality firsthand. You've been forced to grow up today in ways that aren't fair to you. You had to do that last year, too."

I looked at Mr. T's dented head and saw myself throwing that snowball again.

"There's no denying it," Mr. T went on, "you're a special group. I wish I could tell you why all this has happened, but I can't. Someday it might make some sense. I don't know."

If I was so grown up because of all this, I wondered, why couldn't I find the courage to tell my father I didn't want to go to that boarding school?

Alexia

Like, it was a no-brainer. As soon as school was over, I jumped on my bike and pedaled to the Old Woods hangout. I'd been going there pretty regularly. I needed to talk to somebody about my day, and I knew there wouldn't be anyone at home.

I walked in and found Reena and Lisa busy doing homework—the usual. They were always doing homework, ever since school started. They were both taking accelerated classes. Brandon wasn't around because he was at football practice, but he would show up later to give the girls a ride.

"Done!" Reena said, slamming down her pen. She pulled out a cigarette and lit up. Then she passed the lighter to Lisa. I didn't want to smoke, so I jumped right in telling my story, hoping they wouldn't make me take a puff.

"You guys are never gonna believe what happened today!" I said.

"Oh, yeah, 'cause kindergarten is so unbelievable," Reena said. "Sit down, Little Brat. You need to chill. A smoke will take that edge off."

My plan didn't work. I sat down 'cause Reena told me to, and she sounded serious. She scared me when she grabbed my arm that time, so like, I didn't mess with her. She passed me a cigarette and lit it for me. I took a puff and coughed. Even though I'd smoked with them a few times, I still wasn't that good at it, and I still didn't like it all that much. It tasted awful. But Reena and Lisa said that everyone smoked because it helped you chill. Apparently, high school was full of stress.

"You're gonna need this once you join the big girls. Trust me," Reena said.

"I like your lipstick," Lisa said. I was wearing the dark maroon color that she had given me. I smiled. "You look grown up."

I liked Lisa. She was nice and beautiful, and she had a boyfriend. I wanted to be like her.

"Yeah, the boys were probably all over you today, huh," Reena teased. "You cute little thing."

I didn't know how much I liked Reena. She was nice and mean at the same time.

"So what's up with your parents, Lexie? They don't care if you wear lipstick and hang out here?" Reena wanted to know.

I shrugged. "Mom threw Dad out of the house a while ago, so he's out of the picture," I answered. I took another puff. "And Mom's usually asleep when I leave for school in the morning, and she doesn't get home from work until late."

"You're on your own a lot, then," Reena said. "That's pretty grown up for a kindergartner."

"I'm not in kindergarten! I'm in sixth grade!" I yelled.

"Simmer down," Reena said. Then she laughed. "You need to chill."

I must have been chill to spill my guts to them like that. Maybe the cigarettes were working? Not! I blurted out everything because I was sick of Reena's mouth and I was trying to impress them.

"What grade are you guys in?" I asked.

"Tenth," Lisa said, "except Brandon. He's a junior. But don't start worrying about us. Tell us what happened today."

I told my story. They sat and listened and didn't say anything. For once, Reena didn't open her smart mouth. Not until I was done, at least.

"That's the most messed-up story I've ever heard," Reena said.

"Sad," Lisa said softly, shaking her head.

"C'mon, let's blow this joint," Brandon said. I didn't even know he was there. He must have just showed up.

Lisa got to her feet in a flash and took Brandon's arm. "Bye, Lexie."

"See ya, Little Brat," Reena said.

I left right after them. Brandon gave me a thumbs-up as they pulled away in his black car. I watched them leave. His tires spit gravel everywhere when he stomped on the gas and did a nasty fishtail out of the driveway onto Old Woods Road. The car wasn't anything special, but it got them where they were going, and it definitely gave Brandon a power trip.

Danielle

Rescuing a baby. Who's ever heard of that? Maybe of rescuing an animal, but not a baby. There was a time this summer when Charlie and I had to rescue one of our calves. It was a hot, sunny day. We were on our way to the barn to get ready for the evening milking when we heard it, just like Jeffrey said he heard the crying—we heard the bleating. The calf's cries for help came from the pasture. Charlie and I looked and saw the vultures circling out in the distance. They were closing in. We ran across the fields (the same fields some stranger had walked over). When we came over the knoll, we found our newest calf stuck in a mudhole. He must have been trying to cool off or get a drink. Now he couldn't get out, and the more he fought, the deeper he sank. He was chest deep, and completely exhausted.

"We need the truck," Charlie said. "You stay here while I

go get it; otherwise those vultures will have his eyes pecked out before I get back."

I tried to comfort the calf while Charlie was away, same as Jeffrey had tried to soothe the baby. It wasn't easy, and it didn't feel like it was working, but it was all I could do. When Charlie came back, he tied some rope to the rear of his truck. Then he laid some boards across the mud so he could walk out to the calf. He tied the other end of the rope around the little guy's body. The boards also gave the calf something solid to walk on. Then Charlie told me to get in the truck and ease it forward. One of the things you get to do on farms is drive before you get a license. I had driven around the lots before, but I was nervous behind the wheel this time. I let off the pedal gently and cringed when I heard the calf bellowing behind me. But Charlie kept barking words of encouragement, so I inched forward little by little, and eventually we freed him. Back at the barn, we cleaned the calf and got him hydrated, just like the paramedics did with that baby.

We saved him. I can remember how I felt that afternoon—scared, nervous, worried, relieved. That calf, Rupert we named him, is my favorite. He made it. I hope that baby makes it. I can only imagine how Jeffrey must feel.

I told Grandma about the baby when I got home. I ended up telling everyone at dinner, but Grandma was the first person I saw when I got off the bus that day. And that story wasn't the sort of thing I could keep to myself. I found Grandma on her hands and knees in the garden. She kept pulling weeds while I got all the words out. Then she sat up and wiped the sweat from her brow with her already dirty handkerchief. She'd been working all day. She and Grandpa never slowed down.

"Danielle, I don't recall school bein' so unbelievable when I was there. Course, not much about your school is like mine was, but still, I don't think I've ever heard of children havin' the kind of days you seem to have in that room with Mr. Terupt."

"What do you mean?"

"Well, this isn't exactly the sort of stuff that happens in school—teachers almost dying and abandoned babies being rescued. Heck, I don't remember much of anything from my schooling days, 'cept gettin' rapped on the knuckles with a ruler when I didn't do as I was told. I got to think the good Lord has something planned out for you kids in that classroom, 'cause these aren't simple things you're experiencin'."

Mr. Terupt had said something similar. We'd been forced to grow up, and we were certainly a special group because of all we had gone through together. I figured if I could handle the truth about a little baby after watching him almost die, then I ought to be able to know about the man who walked across our fields. I told Grandma as much.

"Danielle, sometimes ignorance is bliss. Do you know what that means?"

"No, ma'am."

"It means you get away without needing to worry so much when you don't know or understand all the details about something. And that's good, 'cause you don't need to be worrying all the time. The adults can do that."

"If I'm experiencing such grown-up things in school, I think I ought to be able to deal with them at home." My voice rose more than I meant it to. "And besides," I added, "I'm already worrying about it."

"Then stop," Grandma demanded, the gentleness in her voice gone. She threw her weeds down and stood up. "There's nothing you can do about it if I do tell ya, so I don't see any point in tellin' ya. And that's the end of it."

"Yes, ma'am." I didn't like her answer one bit, but I didn't talk back. I knew not to push Grandma's buttons. She wasn't going to bend—not today, anyway. I dropped my bag and got down on my hands and knees and started pulling some weeds. I yanked at the green shoots hard enough that my hands started to burn.

"Danielle," Grandma said after some silent weeding. "How's that baby doing?"

"I'm not sure."

"We best pray for him tonight."

"Yes, ma'am."

"And Jeffrey too," Grandma said.

I nodded.

Dear God,

Jeffrey carried a baby into our classroom this morning. A baby that was thrown away. Dropped in the weeds and left there to die. Mr. Terupt did all he could to help, then the ambulance came and took the baby away. Please take care of him. Don't let him die. Jeffrey was his savior, but I'm sure he needs your comfort now, too.

God, I'm not sure why such terrible things need to happen in this world. And at this point, I don't think I'll ever have an answer. But I do know that whoever threw a little baby away like that, must also really need your help. So I want to pray for those people, too. Please help them find the right path. Amen.

Oh, and one last thing. I'd still like it if you could help me find out the truth about that man who was in our fields this summer, but don't tell Grandma. Thank you. Amen.

Jeffrey

Terupt offered to take me to the hospital with him and Ms. Newberry the next day after school. He was going to check on the baby. Everyone wanted to know how he was doing, and I think Terupt sensed that I especially wanted to know. I couldn't think about anything else. But I had to say "No thanks" to his offer. Hospitals still brought back too many bad memories for me, and I just knew that baby would have more tubes and machines hooked up to him than I could handle. I couldn't do it.

After visiting, Terupt reported to our class that the baby was in intensive care. It's a good thing I didn't go with him, because intensive care means lots of tubes and machines. The baby was dehydrated to the point that his kidneys were having problems. He needed special monitoring, so it wasn't a good time for visitors anyway.

Terupt kept in touch with the hospital so he could up-date us on the baby. I hated to think I was getting good at this hoping-for-people-in-hospitals-to-recover-and-not-die thing, but I sure felt like I'd done a lot of it. I didn't stop doing it either. I hoped and hoped for that baby, and by the end of the month, things looked better for him. He had gained some weight, which I'd been told was a good sign for a newborn. Terupt told us that it looked like they'd be moving him to a local medical center soon. He said the doctors thought he'd be at the medical center while the search for his parents continued. The police still hadn't found his mom and dad, and if that didn't change, Terupt told us the baby might go up for adoption.

That was good news, but scary, too. Once I heard the word *adoption*, I was struck by an urgent need to see him.

october

LUKE

I was the first one to submit a formal *Westing Game* solution. I remember the morning I figured it out. I was up early reading what Mr. Terupt had assigned when all of a sudden some of the author's clues came together for me, and bam! I had it! I ran into Mom and Dad's bedroom to celebrate.

"I've got it! I've got it! I've solved it!" I danced and jumped around while they burrowed under the covers, trying to sleep.

"Good. Great, Luke," Dad said from under the blankets.

"We're proud of you, honey," Mom said, peeking out at me.

"Now let us sleep some more," Dad added. He moaned and turned over.

I sat down at the kitchen table and wrote up my conclusion. I stuffed it in an envelope, sealed it, and signed my name across the back.

Detective Luke

I couldn't wait to get to school that morning. I ran into our classroom and handed Mr. Terupt the envelope. Everyone was shocked.

"You've solved it already?" Mr. Terupt said, standing up from his chair, his eyes bugged out and eyebrows raised. He still hadn't turned in a solution. Suddenly he wobbled a bit. He grabbed his desk and closed his eyes for a moment.

"Stood up too fast," he said, after regaining his balance. Then he moved on like nothing had happened. "I'm impressed, especially since I'm not even close to a solution," Mr. Terupt admitted. "But we still don't know if you're right."

"Oh, I'm right," I said.

"I only know of one person who's ever cracked this case before the author reveals the truth, so if you're right, you'll join special company," Mr. Terupt said.

"I'm right," I said.

OBSERVATION
—Mr. Terupt has had two dizzy spells.

QUESTIONS
—Who's the one person that cracked the case?
—Is Mr. Terupt okay?

Detective Luke

Peter

I read *The Westing Game* but never handed in a solution. It was part of my plan to have Mr. T fail me. But I wanted to read the book because I didn't want to miss out. I liked it, a lot, but it's not the story I remember most. It's the drama around the book that's stuck with me, like the day Mr. T turned in his solution.

Mr. T loved to scare the snot out of us whenever we were busy doing something. One time we were taking a timed test and he yelled out "TIME!" after the forty-five minutes were up. A few of us were so rattled we accidentally threw our pencils. Ben banged his legs on the underside of his desk, he jumped so bad. Mr. T laughed his head off, and we laughed with him. So it shouldn't have been a surprise that he made his *Westing Game* announcement during silent reading time.

It was so quiet you'd definitely know where a fart came

from if someone were to let one go, unless, of course, you were the evil Lexie. Suddenly, out of nowhere, Mr. T shouted, "THAT'S IT!" He successfully scared the snot out of us again.

"You might as well call it quits," he announced. "I've got my solution right here and there's no way I'm going to lose. I've solved it."

"Too bad Luke's already turned his in," I said. "Looks like you'll have to settle for second place."

Luke didn't say anything, but Mr. T made a grand production out of adding his envelope to the submission box. He flew it up and down like an airplane, sound effects included, before spinning around and slam-dunking it home.

We were supposed to go back to silent reading. I tried, but it was hard to settle down after Mr. T got us riled up like that. He made everything loads of fun.

Jessica

FADE IN: LS of everyone sitting in their chairs. They've been arranged in a semicircle facing the front of the room, making it a stage area. Written on the board are the words *Solution Opening Ceremony*. MR. TERUPT carries a shoe box in his hands along with his copy of *The Westing Game*. The box holds our solutions.

JESSICA VO

There was nervous chatter among my classmates as Mr. Terupt approached with the solutions, except for me and Luke. We were the only ones not talking while we waited for Mr. Terupt to get ready. Luke was all business. We were anxious, in it together, and hoping to be the winner.

CUT TO: Days earlier in the classroom, during silent reading time. LUKE kneels next to JESSICA in a corner of the room where she's working. THEY talk in hushed voices.

LUKE

How close are you?

JESSICA

I don't know. I'm trying to be patient, hoping that something comes to me, but it's not. I don't know what I'm missing.

LUKE

I wasn't patient. I rushed my solution because I was sure I had it solved, but now I know there's more to it.

LUKE looks down at the floor.

LUKE

I want to tell you what I know, and see if it helps you. Mr. Terupt said only one person has ever solved it, so I want to see if I can help you figure it out—it's too late for me.

LUKE looks up and meets JESSICA's smile.

CUT TO: Solution Opening Ceremony.

MR. TERUPT

Okay, gang. Here's the deal. It's time for us to finish this magnificent riddle. The recommender of this story did not lie—it's a brilliant tale. After we're finished I'll take each solution out one at a time and read it aloud. The one that is most accurate and thorough will be considered the best, with any ties going to the earliest submission. Got it?

Students nod, books at the ready.

CUT TO: MR. TERUPT reading aloud the end of *The Westing Game* and the class following along in their copies. Signs of shock and disbelief are seen throughout the students. We see mouths agape and heads shaking. PETER smacks his forehead.

PETER
(excited, springing up in his seat)
Holy smokes! If anybody got that, then they're wicked smart!

CUT TO: MEDIUM SHOT (MS) of MR. TERUPT. He starts pulling envelope after envelope from the box and reading the answers out loud. Then he gets to Luke's and holds it up for the class to see. CLOSE-UP (CU) of the envelope. DETECTIVE LUKE is scrawled across the seal. MR. TERUPT opens it and reads LUKE's solution aloud.

MR. TERUPT
(after whistling)
Very impressive, Luke. Your solution is certainly evidence of a detective in the making.

JEFFREY
Way to go, Lukester.

LUKE shrugs. Then he glances at JESSICA, who's trying to be sneaky by not looking back at him.

I liked Mr. Terupt for praising Luke when he knew his own solution was better. But he hadn't opened my envelope yet, and he didn't know that Luke had a hand in that solution, too.

CUT TO: CU of the next envelope. We see MR. TERUPT's name. He opens it and reads his solution to a silent audience.

MR. TERUPT
(flexing his muscles)
It seems I was right, Peter. I'm sorry, but my solution happens to be the best.

LUKE
(raising his finger in the air)
Not so fast. Let's not forget, we still have Jessica's.

There is wild cheering now. A chant begins.

CLASS
Jessica . . . Jessica . . . Jessica . . .

CUT TO: CU of MR. TERUPT smiling. Pull back as he opens the last envelope—JESSICAS's—and reads her solution.

JESSICA VO
I shouldn't have been surprised when Luke offered to help. He was the one who let me borrow snow pants last winter,

on the day of the accident. He did his best to help Mr. Terupt when he fell in the snow. And on that final day in the Collaborative Classroom, Luke and James helped all of us tell Peter the accident wasn't only his fault. Luke was someone you could count on—he'd be there for you.

MR. TERUPT looks up after finishing JESSICA's solution.

MR. TERUPT

Well, there's no doubt about it. We've found our winner. Congratulations, Jessica. Come on up here and get your award.

CUT TO: Everyone cheering. JESSICA stands and walks over to LUKE. They slap each other five. Then JESSICA walks up to MR. TERUPT.

MR. TERUPT
(to the class)

I present to you our winner of the *Westing Game* Competition, Miss Jessica. Her award is a gift card to Snow Hill Bookshop.

More cheering from the class.

JESSICA
(still onstage, facing Mr. Terupt)

Mr. Terupt, you taught us that we do better when we stick together. And, well, I couldn't have won the competition without Luke's help. He deserves this award as much as I do.

MR. TERUPT
(to all)

It takes a special person to admit that, Jessica. And it takes a special person to help out a friend. Luke, please come up here and receive your gift card. I just happen to have one for you.

LUKE stands and walks to the front, joining JESSICA. MR. TERUPT hands him the gift card, then sweeps his arm in a gesture to present the winners. There is a standing ovation. LUKE and JESSICA shake hands.

CUT TO: Class back in their seats and MR. TERUPT still standing at the stage area. LUKE raises his hand.

MR. TERUPT

Yes, Luke.

LUKE

Who was the *one* person to actually solve the mystery before the book revealed it?

MR. TERUPT

Ah, yes. The recommender of this book was also the person who solved it—my mother.

FADE OUT.

JESSICA VO

Luke and I came close with our solution. It may have been the best in the class, but we still didn't have it completely figured out. There was more to Sam Westing than we had realized. We didn't really know him—just like we didn't really know our teacher. Mr. Terupt was our very own Sam Westing, and my desire to find out more about him was stronger now than ever.

Peter

After we wrapped up the Solution Opening Ceremony, Mr. T asked his book team (me and Anna) to return the books to the library. It was the perfect opportunity to try my stacking method again.

"Peter, just let me carry some," Anna insisted.

"No," I said. I was determined to show her I could do it. "I've got it this time. Just lead the way so I don't run into anything." That's the only thing I was worried about.

I held a forty-book tower. That was more copies of *The Westing Game* than we needed, but we had extras so we could keep one at home, plus I had a few library books that needed returning. I pressed my hands on the ends of the stack, leaving myself wide open. I started to follow Anna. I had everything under control until Jeffrey decided it was time to get even. He shot me in the front of my pants with several water blasts from the lizards' spray bottle.

"Hey!" I yelled.

Anna gasped.

"What's wrong?" Mr. T wanted to know.

"Nothing," I said. "We're all set." I didn't want to turn around so everyone could see my wet private area.

"Told you to grow eyes in the back of your head," Jeffrey whispered. "Now we're even."

He went back to spraying the bog and I followed Anna out of the classroom. Now I was even more determined to succeed with my book tower. My wet pants had to be worth something.

I repositioned the books so I had one hand by my chin and the other down below my belt. It was easier for me to see, and I felt in control. Plus, I had myself protected now.

"I knew I could do it," I said.

"We're not there yet," Anna said. "Don't jinx yourself."

I was hurrying as fast as I could because I wanted to get to the library before anything bad happened.

"Walk!" Mrs. Williams's voice scared me worse than Mr. T's stunt during silent reading. My tower of books shot out all over the place and then this little twerp came flying by us down the hall.

"Oh, Peter. I'm sorry," Mrs. Williams said. "I didn't mean to scare you. I was trying to get that kindergartner to stop running." She bent down to pick up some of the books. "Oh, heavens!" she said as she spotted my overly wet pants. "I'm really very sorry. I didn't mean to scare you like *that*."

Great, I thought. Mrs. Williams thinks I wet myself out of fright. Just what I wanted.

Anna started turning red from holding her breath. I

could tell she was about to lose it and sure enough she burst out laughing. It was ridiculous.

I picked up a pile of books and carried them into the library. I didn't even bother trying another tower. I left the rest for Anna. I just needed to get out of there.

LUKE

We had just finished our work with *The Westing Game* when Mr. Terupt introduced our next major task. October was a month for surprises.

"Research, gang. I think it's time we tackle a research project," he said, standing at the front of the room.

I liked it. But what would I research?

"What do you mean, project?" Tommy asked.

"Well, instead of simply writing papers, I thought we'd try developing PowerPoint presentations. We can share them with each other, and maybe some other people too."

Awesome! Classic Mr. Terupt.

Everyone got excited and started talking about ideas, so I'm not sure if anyone else saw his spell. Mr. Terupt closed his eyes and leaned on the front table until he felt steady again. Then he continued—as if nothing had happened.

"You can choose to work alone or with a partner," Mr. Terupt said. He went on to explain more, but my wheels were already spinning.

I was eager to get started right away with this new project, and I knew exactly what my topic would be. Mr. Terupt's bouts of dizziness and light-headedness were bugging me. I didn't like that he was having them. I wasn't sure if there was anything to these observations or not, so that's why I decided to research post–head trauma complications and side effects. I needed to make sure Mr. Terupt was okay.

QUESTION
—Is there a link between Mr. Terupt's spells and his head trauma?

Detective Luke

Alexia

Like, Jessica didn't give me much time to think about that research thing. She asked me if I wanted to be her partner that very day. Like I'd ever say no to her when it came to working on a project.

"Lexie, I've got a great idea for the research project. Want to do it with me?"

We were sitting at a table in the caf eating our lunches. Danielle and Anna were sitting with us, but they were busy talking about something else. Maybe that was why Jessica asked me—'cause I was just chillin'.

"What's your idea?" I asked her.

"I want to research making movies."

Like, what was I supposed to say? I didn't know anything about making movies, so I was quiet. I think Jessica thought my silence meant that, like, I wasn't excited about her idea.

"It'll be great! You can focus on costume and wardrobe design," Jessica said. "You can even dress up as a fancy actress for our presentation."

I raised my eyebrows. That was sounding better. Jessica could tell I was warming to the idea. She smiled.

Basically, I wanted to stick with Jessica for a partner. I knew she'd do all sorts of research, and I could just sort of tag along. I wasn't exactly using her. It wasn't like I wanted her to do *all* the work, but she wouldn't care. And I had other things to worry about, like getting to the hangout after school. I thought about that all the time.

"Hey, Little Brat. Good to see ya, girl," Reena said when I walked into the back room of the abandoned house that afternoon. She always greeted me like that.

"Have we got a surprise for you today!" Lisa said.

They must not have had a lot of homework. Usually I like surprises, but I was nervous about this one. I should have seen that as a warning sign.

"Enough of the cutesy animal stuff and pretty pink hearts, Little Brat. We're gonna make a woman out of you," Reena said.

Suddenly, I felt like *their* little project, but I went along with them—again. Lisa and Reena had all sorts of hand-me-down clothes and accessories for me. I love clothes, so I stopped feeling nervous. I thought of it as my wardrobe research. They helped me pick out an outfit and I hurried into one of the other rooms and tried it on.

"Now, that's hot," Lisa said, pointing to me when I came back in. I was wearing black yoga pants and a camouflage top. I used a matching camo scrunchie to hold back my hair.

"That's fresh," Reena said. "Camo's hot."

"You look older now," Lisa said.

I smiled. I did feel older in the clothes, and hanging out with Lisa and Reena. How couldn't I feel that way after going to school with Boy Scout Luke? He'd actually worn his Boy Scout shirt to school that day—the dork! If anyone needed wardrobe help, it was Luke. But I was the one who knew how to appreciate these clothes.

"I thought you meant she looked hot *for real*," Brandon said as he walked in and plunked down on the sofa.

What was he doing here? Why wasn't he at football practice?

"You know, after all that pedaling," he said. "Here, have a drink, Lex." He handed me his bottled water. That was when I noticed his other arm in a cast.

"What happened?" I said.

"Broke it during our last game. I've got a metal plate and eight screws in there now." He paused. "That means no more football," he said with his voice lowered, "and kiss wrestling season good-bye too." Brandon shook his head. "It really sucks. But, hey, guess I can party it up now. So take a drink, little Lexie!"

I *was* hot for real. Plus, I felt bad for Brandon. I didn't know what to say or do, so I took a big gulp from his bottle— and spit the firewater all over the room. If I thought my chest burned after my first cigarette, let me tell you, I was wrong. My mouth and throat were torched from that swallow. Brandon was practically rolling around on the floor he was laughing so hard. He reminded me of Peter after he hit me with that flying cardboard square the day we were counting blades of grass with Teach. Like Peter, Brandon thought he was sooo funny.

"That was mean, Brandon," Lisa said.

"But funny," he said.

"What is that!" I yelled.

"Vodka," Brandon said. "Teachers think they're so smart, but they're so easy to trick. All I do is put vodka in a water bottle and I can go all day without them even knowing what I'm really drinking. Fools!"

Not Teach, I thought. You couldn't fool him. Thinking of Teach suddenly made me feel uneasy.

"Well, like, I can't stay today," I lied. "My mom is gonna be home early, so I need to get going."

"What are you talking about!" Brandon demanded. He punched the sofa, got up, and started pacing. "You don't need to go anywhere. It's party time."

He was mad all of a sudden. And I was scared. His temper reminded me of my dad's.

"Let her go," Lisa said.

Brandon spun to face Lisa, and I quickly made my move to leave.

"Shut up!" I heard him yelling.

I ran outside, jumped on my bike, and pedaled as fast as I could to get away from the hangout. Behind me, I heard Brandon's car start up. I got off the road and hid. When I looked back, I saw the dust flying from his famous fishtail exit as he sped away in the other direction.

Danielle

I had a hard time thinking about anything other than that man in our fields. Grandma told me ignorance is bliss, but that didn't stop me from worrying. I already knew too much. I saw how upset my family was that night in the kitchen. I saw how stressed my grandpa continued to be. And I saw my grandmother's growing concern over my stressed-out grandfather. Grandpa didn't have time for small talk at the dinner table anymore. He talked less and less, and seemed to be looking out the window more and more—looking for that man in our fields, I knew. There was silent talk between Mom and Grandma, their eyes darting back and forth across the table. And I was supposed to be ignorant? Not a chance.

I read *The Westing Game* like Mr. Terupt wanted, but I just didn't have the mind energy to try and solve the mystery like he had hoped. And I couldn't come up with something for the new PowerPoint project. I wanted to research an answer about the man in our fields, but I didn't know what question to ask in order to get a presentation out of that. So I was topicless, but I wasn't the only one. Peter was without a topic too. Mr. Terupt pulled us aside one day and asked us what we thought about researching drugs.

"What do you mean, drugs?" I asked.

"I mean the bad ones," Mr. Terupt said. "The ones you hear about in the news, and will hear about all too soon in school. The ones you and your friends might be asked to try someday."

Peter and I were quiet. What did Mr. Terupt mean, "asked to try"? I wasn't ever going to do any drugs. I didn't even know what that meant, but I knew it was bad. And that was when I realized I didn't know much of anything about drugs. I was beginning to understand why Mr. Terupt thought it could be a good topic.

"You want us to learn about some of the bad drugs, what they could do to us, and . . . what else?" I said.

"Well, first I just wanted to see what you thought about the topic," Mr. Terupt said. "If you're okay with it, I'll let you get started. Then I'll check back with you after you've done some work, and I'll help you get more focused with your research."

I looked at Peter and all he did was shrug, so I said, "Okay, we'll do it."

"Great," Mr. Terupt said. "Snow Hill School doesn't have a formal drug education program like D.A.R.E., so I know we'll learn a lot from you guys. And it's going to be really important."

"Look, Danielle," Peter said when Mr. Terupt walked away. "I'll help you with the research because I'll feel bad if I make you do all of it alone, but I can't help you with the actual PowerPoint stuff."

"Why not?"

"I just can't."

"What if I tell Mr. Terupt?" I said. I wasn't really going to be a tattletale, but I threatened it anyway.

Peter started to say something, but then stopped. He was thinking. Then he surprised me. "Go right ahead," he said. "Tell him."

Peter did just what he said he'd do. He helped gather information, and he did zero work on the computer. But I didn't rat on him. I didn't have to. Mr. Terupt knew something was up. He told me so.

Dear God,

Ignorance might be bliss, but I'm not ignorant about that man in our fields. I'm even worrying about him, despite Grandma's wishes. I pray you can help me get some answers, and I pray for Grandpa, who looks too stressed these days. Please provide comfort for my family. And God, I think you should check in on Peter. I'm not sure what he's up to, but he might need some guidance. Amen.

Jeffrey

I can tell you this. When you rescue a baby from a shoe box, it's not something you forget. And when you go home every day to a house that's silent, you have even more time to think about the baby you saved.

"Have you come up with anything yet?" Terupt asked me one day in the library. We were down there for our research projects, either getting books for the topic we were going to research or, in my case, looking at books to try and come up with a topic.

"No," I said.

"What do you want to do?"

"I don't know."

"Oh, come on!" Terupt said. "What's on your mind? There must be something you're thinking about these days."

He knew exactly what that something was.

Once the baby was moved from the hospital to the center in New Haven, I started going to see him. The building was huge. It stretched out in all different directions, a lot like our school. It was a place for physical and occupational therapy and rehabilitation. I wasn't exactly sure what all that meant, but the entire complex was called Center for Love and Care.

It was a downhill ride from our school into New Haven. Biking there was smooth sailing, but coming back wasn't so easy. I didn't let that stop me, though—I still went. I had to see him.

The nurses in the center named him Asher. I liked it. They picked the name because it meant *lucky*. I wasn't sure how lucky the little guy really was, though. Officer Stoneley still had no leads about the mother or father. The investigation remained open, but not hopeful. I also knew having a mother and father didn't automatically make everything perfect, either.

"What is it, Jeffrey?" Mr. Terupt asked. "Or should I say, who is it?"

"Asher," I said. "I think about him all the time. There. Are you happy now?" I shoved the book I was holding back onto the shelf. "And there's no way for me to research *him*, is there?"

"Don't get upset, Jeffrey. I know he's on your mind. He's on all our minds," Terupt said. "So how do you make him work for the project?"

"What?" I said. "I can't. I just told you that."

"Why not? I bet you can find lots to research based on

your observations and the questions you have. Trust me," Terupt said. "Then you can include some personal anecdotes, which will really liven up your presentation. Anecdotes are little stories that go along with your talk—they'd be real stories from your actual visits."

"But the weather's beginning to make it harder for me to go to the center every day," I said.

Terupt frowned. "Well, if getting there is the only hurdle, let's think about what we can do."

"I can help," Anna said. She was on the other side of the shelf, also looking through books to find a topic. She must have heard us talking. We looked at her. "My mom gets out of her school when we do. She'd pick us up and give us a ride."

That's how I ended up doing my research project with Anna. It was that simple.

anna

Mom picked us up in the car after school. Jeffrey told us how to get to the medical center. I couldn't believe he'd been biking such a long way. But I wasn't surprised. Mom walked in with me and Jeffrey, and he introduced us to Nurse Barry. Mr. Terupt had called ahead and explained our research project to her. It was agreed that Jeffrey would continue to spend time with Asher and that I would help out in other parts of the center.

Nurse Barry was very welcoming. She gave me and Mom the grand tour while Jeffrey rushed off to find Asher.

One area of the center, where Asher was staying, was dedicated to children (the pediatric wing), and an area on the other side of the building was for old people (the geriatric wing). Nurse Barry passed us off to Nurse Rose in the geriatric wing, and Mom and I spent the rest of our first visit with her. We helped her with Barney, an elderly man who was recovering from a stroke. I didn't know anything about rehabilitation or physical or occupational therapy, and before that afternoon I didn't have any old people in my life (just Danielle's grandparents, and they didn't like me, so I didn't count them), but I soon found out I liked all of the above. And so did my mom.

Barney struggled with partial paralysis, which means he had lost the use of one side of his body. That's something that can happen as a result of a stroke. I included information on strokes in my presentation. I learned a lot about them, and heart attacks, too. Mom and I continued to work with Barney for several weeks. We helped him use his walker until he regained his strength and could walk on his own two feet again. It felt great!

"You really like helping all those old farts and senile geezers?" Peter joked after hearing me talk about my visits. He sounded like it was hard for him to believe.

"Yes," I said. "I do."

"Cool." Peter didn't say anything more. He could tell I was serious.

"And she's great at it," Jeffrey added. "I've seen her in action."

I smiled. Jeffrey was right. I *was* great at it.

november

Jessica

FADE IN: There is a knock at the door, and in walks MRS. WILLIAMS. We see her look at the floor and gingerly walk across it, obviously making sure she doesn't slip and crash-land with her underwear showing like last year.

MR. TERUPT
(at the front of the room)
Okay, gang. Mrs. Williams is here with an important announcement, so please give her your attention.

MR. TERUPT walks over to his desk, once again stopping to hold on to it for a few seconds before sitting down.

CUT TO: MRS. WILLIAMS standing at the front of the room.

JESSICA VO

We saw a lot of Mrs. Williams. Between last year and Jeffrey showing up with a baby this year, we'd been through a lot with her. We were special to her, and she had become special to us. That's one of the things that can happen when you go through a tragedy together—everyone involved ends up closer. But for Mr. Terupt to take the time to formally get our attention, and for him to call Mrs. Williams's news "an important announcement," suggested something serious. I had no idea what was coming.

MRS. WILLIAMS

Good morning, everyone. It's always nice to come and see this class. I'm here to tell you that Snow Hill School has been awarded a grant for what is best described as an exchange program. The state has awarded us money to use toward collaboration with the other sixth grades in our region. You will be getting together with the students from Woods View School two or three times this year.

LUKE lets out a sigh in exasperation. He gets surprised looks from many in the room after his out-of-character reaction.

MRS. WILLIAMS

The first get-together will be in just a couple of weeks. At that time you'll be required to work on projects in groups. Your groups should be made up of a few of you with a few of them.

LUKE
(not thrilled)
Why does the state want to pay for that?

MRS. WILLIAMS
Because we're interested in giving you opportunities to meet and make friends with the kids you'll be going to junior high school with next year. The state always likes to promote programs that ask students to work together.

LEXIE
(leaning over to Jessica)
This is our chance to meet some boys.

PETER
(while staring down at his desk, playing with an eraser)
We already work together in this classroom. Why do we have to do it with outsiders?
(under his breath)
It's not like I'll be in school with them next year anyway.

LUKE
What sorts of projects are we talking about?

JEFFREY
(grumbling)
Doesn't matter.

MR. TERUPT gets up from his desk and walks to the front of the room and stands by MRS. WILLIAMS.

MR. TERUPT

Luke, since we're getting money from the state, we can do some bigger projects. You'll like it, trust me. In fact, we're going to be starting an oceanography unit in the next few days, and our first exchange project will be something special to go along with that.

LUKE's face brightens. He rubs his hands together in a way that tells us he can't wait to get started.

LUKE
(excited)

Oceanography! Awesome! I've been thinking I might want to study marine science when I get older. Can you believe only ten percent of the world's oceans have been explored? There's all kinds of observations and discoveries waiting to be made!

CLASS laughs at LUKE's dorky energy and excitement.

LUKE

What?! I'm serious. I've been swimming a lot this last month to earn my Athletics Badge. You have to be a good swimmer if you want to explore the ocean.

LEXIE

Oh boy! Do you think you can wear that really cool Boy Scout shirt again when you get the badge?

LUKE

Sure. Okay.

JESSICA VO

Lexie's sarcasm went right over Luke's head. The poor kid probably *would* wear that ridiculous shirt again. He wasn't always the sharpest knife in the drawer.

MR. TERUPT
(smiling)

Now, gang, remember how scared you were before visiting the Collaborative Classroom last year. This is no different. That turned out to be a great experience, and I'm sure this will too. Be positive.

JESSICA VO

Did Mr. Terupt really believe that? The Collaborative Classroom had been his idea. This was someone else's. Other than Lexie, I'm not sure any of us were excited. I know the boys weren't, that was easy to see, though Luke did perk up at the prospect of bigger projects.

MRS. WILLIAMS
(trying to appear confident)

Mr. Terupt's right. Let's be positive. I'm sure things will turn out differently than you expect.

MRS. WILLIAMS smiles and walks to the door. She stops and turns to wave.

MRS. WILLIAMS

Have a great day, everyone.

CLASS

Bye, Mrs. Williams. You too.

JESSICA VO

I was feeling overwhelmed. I still wanted to learn more about Mr. Terupt, our very own Sam Westing, plus I had my research project to think about. My partner had me concerned. Lexie had gone from a normal-dressing sixth grader to a high school–looking girl with real lipstick and a "chill" vocabulary. She claimed it was part of her wardrobe research. She was learning how to be an actress. I think she was getting her information from the supermarket tabloids. I have a strong command of language, but even I hadn't heard some of her words before, at least not how she was using them. Now, on top of all that, there was the exchange program to worry about. No wonder I had a lot on my mind.

FADE OUT.

Alexia

I was looking hot. Totally. With these other sixth graders coming to visit, I was like, girl, you need to look your best. I wore my black yoga pants with a purple scoop-neck sweater that Lisa had given me. Lisa and Reena made me ditch the feather boas I loved to wear last year a while ago. They gave me a couple of scarves instead. According to them, scarves were the bomb in accessories. I wore the one that had some purple in it and I put on my favorite lipstick and some mascara. To put the finishing touches on my outfit, I added silver hoop earrings. Reena and Lisa would have approved.

That morning in school, I like, sized myself up in the girls' bathroom. I was standing sideways looking in the mirror when Jessica walked in.

"Hi, Lexie."

"Hey, girlfriend."

"You're looking . . . nice and grown up," she said.

"Nah. I need something more. I have to look amazing today. We've got visitors coming." Jessica watched as I checked myself out. "I need more of a chest," I said. "That's what this sweater is all about."

"What?" Jessica sounded shocked. I heard it in her voice. I loved it when I got to teach *her* something for a change.

"I need boobs," I said. "Grab me some toilet paper, wouldja. And don't be stingy. Get a lot." I was tired of waiting for them to grow on their own.

Jessica brought me the goods. "What are you going to do?"

"Just watch," I said. I wadded the toilet paper, pulled up my sweater, and stuffed my bra, first one side, then the other. I tried to even things out in the mirror. I cupped and squeezed and formed a nice pair. "Are they even?" I spun around.

"What?!" Jessica was even more shocked now.

"Jessica. Girlfriend." I put my hand on her shoulder. "We can do yours too if you want."

"No," she said, taking a step back. "That's okay."

"Just tell me. Are they even?"

"Yes." She paused for a second. "They look . . . fine."

I inspected myself in the mirror again. "No," I said. "They're too small. I need boobs, not boobies. Grab me some more toilet paper, wouldja?"

"I'd be careful not to make it too obvious," Jessica warned. "No bosom yesterday and suddenly a plentiful bosom today doesn't exactly add up."

"It's no sweat. Nobody in our class will say anything. And like, our visitors won't know the difference. To them, I'll just be the hot girl." I cupped and squeezed. "How do they look now?" I spun around again.

"Abundant."

Peter

I remember my brother telling me a long time ago that the kids from Woods View School always think they're better than us. That was why I wasn't real excited for this day. None of us were, except Lexie. One look at her and I knew she was looking forward to it. One look at her and I forgot all about my nervousness. She had definitely put time into getting ready. Her new purple sweater was something. She looked amazing.

"You can pop your eyes back in your head, Peter," Jessica said. "They're not real."

"What? I don't know what you're talking about," I said.

"Lexie's breasts aren't real, Peter. Just thought I'd tell you before you started drooling all over yourself."

Now I was mad. What was I doing gawking at Lexie? And how could I get caught? Lexie was my rival. She was a girl who farted, and there was no way I could like a girl who did that. It was way too gross.

LUKE

I'm sorry to say, but I hypothesized disaster for this exchange program. It was a lot like chemistry. If you take two chemicals and mix them together, what happens? Well, my hypothesis was tested and confirmed at our first Exchange Day. The result was a violent reaction. The data was conclusive. This exchange thing was a bad idea.

"Welcome," Mr. Terupt said as our visitors arrived. "Please, come in and sit down wherever you see an empty seat." He was standing at the front of the room. Once everyone was settled he spoke again.

"W-w-welcome to our sch-sch-school."

What was wrong? Why was Mr. Terupt stuttering? I heard some of the visiting kids snickering and laughing. Laughing at my teacher. I felt hot. Anger surged through my veins.

Before I had time to think about it more, Jeffrey exploded

and tackled the jokester sitting next to him. One of Jeffrey's forearms was planted under the kid's chin and his other one landed right across the chest. He flipped the kid right over the back of his chair. Jeffrey jumped on the boy and pinned him to the ground. Luckily, Mr. Terupt got there just in time to grab Jeffrey before he started throwing punches. And believe me, Jeffrey was ready to let that kid have it good.

I didn't budge. I was silently rooting for Jeffrey. How dare anyone laugh at my teacher.

Jeffrey

First that kid laughed at Terupt. Laughed at my stuttering teacher with his other punk buddies sittin' around my table. Then he said, "What is this guy? A *retard*?"

I didn't even think about it. I just reacted. I wanted to hurt him—bad.

Danielle

"Class meeting," Mr. Terupt announced. Or maybe I should say ordered. Class meetings had always been favorites of mine. The meetings were a chance for us to share our ideas and concerns. But I wasn't sure about this one. I knew Mr. Terupt would have plenty to say. Who could blame him after what Jeffrey did? Speaking of Jeffrey, he wasn't there for this meeting. He was with Mrs. Williams, probably discussing his attack on that boy—a boy I recognized from the summer.

Mr. Terupt had rushed over and pulled Jeffrey off the boy, who stayed on the ground holding his bloody nose. Then Mr. Terupt led Jeffrey out into the hall and came back in without him in less than a minute. I didn't see Jeffrey for the rest of the day.

The visiting teacher was next on the scene. Mrs. Stern

was her name, and stern was her game. One look at her and you knew she meant business. She was old and old-fashioned. I got the feeling she'd still rap you on the knuckles with a ruler. She was one of those teachers Grandma understood.

Mrs. Stern helped her student sit up, but didn't bother showing him any sympathy.

"What did you say this time, Derek?"

"Nothin'," Derek muttered. He cupped his hand under his nose, but I didn't care if he was hurt. Derek was the jerk from the pool—the one who called me a whale.

Marty and Wendy took him down to the nurse to get cleaned up (Nurse Barton was good at that, as I would soon find out), and the rest of us continued with the first Exchange Day.

Mr. Terupt had told us that the projects would be bigger and better because we had gotten money from the state. He wasn't lying. We had a marine biologist come to Snow Hill School to help us perform squid dissections as part of our oceanography unit.

Our art room was converted into a science lab. We crowded around the tables. I was so excited. I love animals—all kinds. I've been thinking about becoming a veterinarian.

Once we were all settled, the guest biologist, Squid Man, took charge. "Today you will be looking at squid. It's very important that you listen and follow directions carefully. We want you to explore, but also learn."

Squid Man said a few more things and then passed out the slimy creatures. Definitely not what I was expecting. A room full of squid has a very strong odor. It's the kind of smell that can make some people nauseated. It didn't bother me. After being around cow poop all my life, I had become used to strong aromas.

"Teach, I'm not—"

That was all Lexie managed to say. The next thing out of her mouth was a stream of barf.

"Eww!" the visitor boys shouted. "Did you see that? The girl with the purple sweater just yakked everywhere." They laughed and cheered and thought it was great.

I felt bad for Lexie but I'm pretty sure she smiled when she heard them mention her purple sweater.

"She ought to take some of that stuffing out of her sweater and clean herself up," Luke whispered.

I looked at him, alarmed and embarrassed. I couldn't talk about that sort of thing with a boy! I couldn't talk about that sort of thing with anyone!

"What?" he said. "Lexie looks like a puffer fish. Any detective can tell she added some fake ones. I don't know much about that sort of thing, but I do know they don't grow like that overnight."

I laughed.

"Do you think Lexie knows puffer fish inflate to scare off predators, not to attract mates?" Luke said.

I laughed again.

Lexie went to Nurse Barton's. The rest of the dissection went smoothly. Mr. Terupt called for the class meeting as soon as our guests were gone.

We had our chairs arranged in a circle, and Mr. Terupt sat down with our microphone. He didn't say a word. Peter held his hand out, and Mr. Terupt gave him the mike.

"Jeffrey wouldn't just do that," Peter said. "That kid had

it coming. I heard them laughing at you, Mr. T, and I'll bet he said something, too."

Anna went next. "I know fighting is wrong, but I think Peter's right. Something happened that made Jeffrey do that."

Then Luke took a turn. "Mr. Terupt, those boys started snickering and laughing when you stuttered. That's probably when that boy said something. Are you all right?"

"I'm fine," Mr. Terupt was quick to say, taking the microphone. "Don't start worrying about me."

When he said that, I thought, Ignorance is bliss. Was this another one of those things an adult didn't want us worrying about? Maybe Mr. Terupt wasn't okay. First he stuttered; then, after he bent down and grabbed Jeffrey under the arms and pulled him up, Mr. Terupt stumbled. Jeffrey actually grabbed ahold of Mr. Terupt to keep him from tripping and falling. Did he just lose his balance or was he dizzy?

"Look, gang," Mr. Terupt said. "I'm really proud of the way you're sticking up for Jeffrey. I'm sure he was provoked. But even so, you can't just lash out and attack others. It could cost you—big-time. You need to learn to handle those situations civilly. You need to always keep control, because to lose it could result in something you don't intend."

"Like a snowball," Peter mumbled.

"Yes, like a snowball," Mr. Terupt said. "I think you get my point."

Later that day I arrived home with lots to talk about again, but that was no surprise to Grandma. I filled her in on the fight and the talk we had with Mr. Terupt.

"We're tryin' to keep it civil, but I don't know how long that's goin' to last," she said.

What was she talking about? My classroom, or something else? The man from our fields?

"What do you mean?" I asked.

"Oh, nothin'. Here." Grandma handed me the peeler and a bowl of potatoes. She grabbed a knife and started dicing up the potatoes she had already peeled. "It's fine to get two different groups of people together, like the state is having your class do with this exchange program," Grandma said, "but if the two sides aren't ready to get along, then you're just askin' for trouble. You can't force that sort of thing. And if you try to"—Grandma looked up from her potatoes and pointed her knife hand at me—"you're gonna get violence." She went back to dicing.

"What could possibly be so hard for people to talk about?" I asked.

"When it gets personal," Grandma said. And then she mumbled something, but I couldn't hear her.

"What did you say?" I asked. I wasn't sure, but I thought she might have said "land."

"Pass me those potatoes you've peeled." Grandma was quick to move past that part of our conversation.

Dear God,

First, let me say thanks. You sure gave that Derek kid a lesson today. I knew you'd get him for me, I just didn't expect to get to see it. That was great! Forgive me for saying that.

God, I suppose ignorance can be bliss, but not if you aren't ignorant, and I'm not. Suddenly I've got more to worry about. Is Mr. Terupt really okay? And is this man-from-our-fields thing going to get violent? Does it have something to do with land? Are you helping me find answers, or just giving me more questions? I need your help, please. Also, I think you better keep an eye on Lexie. Her so-called wardrobe research was a little over the top, on top, today. Amen.

Jeffrey

I got that kid good before I was pulled off him. He thought he could run his mouth in our room. I wasn't gonna sit there and let him crack those jokes. I wouldn't change a thing about what I did. I'd do it all again.

"Jeffrey, what happened?" Mrs. Williams had me in her office. She was fishin' for answers. "What made you lash out like that?"

I stared at the floor. "He was makin' fun of Terupt. Said he was a retard."

"I know how angry that must have made you, but you can't react like that. You've got to control yourself."

Mrs. Williams didn't know how angry that kid made me. She knew I was sensitive about Terupt, like everybody else in my class, and she probably figured I was sensitive to the "retard" comment because of our work with the Collaborative

Classroom last year (which was true), but she knew nothing about Michael, the part of me that was most sensitive to that kid's mouth. She'd never know. But I nodded.

"You know there has to be a consequence."

I nodded again.

"Our school policy is that you must serve a three-day out-of-school suspension for something like this," Mrs. Williams said.

I didn't know it at the time, but that suspension would turn out to be a blessing.

anna

I might not be as good as Luke when it comes to observations, but I don't miss much. Lexie was different. Maybe our exchange guests didn't take notice of her chest, but I sure did. And I know Mr. Terupt did too. Same for all our boys. Peter was bug-eyed from the moment he spotted her. Here I was, always being nice and helpful, and yet I was still invisible. He was more interested in the girl who teased him. The good news was, Lexie got sick so she didn't get to parade around in her new look for very long.

Jessica, Danielle, and I never got around to talking about Lexie because of what happened with Jeffrey and the kid, but I know Mr. Terupt noticed Lexie's other changes, too—like her lipstick and everything-is-chill attitude. So after her stuffed bra, and maybe because of that unbelievable day, Mr. Terupt decided it was time to talk to Lexie.

"Hey, Lex," I heard him say. "I'd like you to hang out for a few minutes after school today so we can talk."

"Gee, Teach. I'd love to, but like, I got someplace I need to be right after school."

"I just need a few minutes, Lex. I'm sure whatever you need to do can wait those few minutes. Don't you think?"

I was waiting for Mom to pick me up after school. Jeffrey was at home serving his suspension so I was going to the center by myself. As it turned out, Mom just happened to be running a few minutes late that day, so I was still there when Mr. Terupt started talking to Lexie.

"Lex, what's up these days? I notice you've replaced the lip gloss with lipstick, the boas with scarves, you have new clothes and new words, and now you're in a big hurry to get out of here after school every day. Where've you been going?"

Lexie shrugged. "Nowhere," she said.

Lie, I thought. She wasn't looking at Mr. Terupt.

I didn't get to hear any more of their talk. Mr. Terupt knew I was eavesdropping and he gave me a look. I moved to the other side of the room, away from them. I stood looking out the windows, waiting for my mom. Lexie ended up leaving before me.

"Anna," Mr. Terupt said, after I spotted Mom and turned to go. "Lexie's your friend."

"Yes," I said. But he didn't say anything else. Ms. Newberry walked into our classroom just then, so I left with a smile, but I was wondering why Mr. Terupt had said that to me.

After our visit to the center that afternoon, Mom decided to drive home a different way. "Where are we going?" I asked.

"Home, but I thought we'd take the scenic route," she said.

What a lucky coincidence that turned out to be. We turned down Old Woods Road and went for a while before passing a run-down, abandoned house. And what did I see lying on the ground next to that old house's front porch?

Lexie's bike.

LUKE

After the episode, and I'm referring to Mr. Terupt's stuttering and stumbling, not Jeffrey's explosion, my research felt urgent. I ended up learning more about post–head trauma than I think I wanted to know.

Simple things like dizzy spells or stuttering can be an indication of some recurring bleeding at the site of an injury. There's also a possibility of seizures. Seizures are a result of sudden, abnormal electrical activity in the brain. There are people who have seizures regularly, but that's because they have a brain disorder called epilepsy. Epilepsy didn't apply to Mr. Terupt, so I didn't spend much time reading about it. However, seizures can also happen to anyone with a problem in the brain, and head trauma can cause a problem. Seizures can last from a few seconds to several minutes, and they can range from mild, which might be Mr. Terupt stopping midsentence and spacing out for a moment, to severe, in which case we would know, because Mr. Terupt would be on the ground, convulsing. Convulsions are when the body shakes out of control. I didn't want that to happen to Mr. Terupt, but if he was already having dizzy spells and stuttering, wasn't this next?

OBSERVATION
—Mr. Terupt is having repeated dizzy spells and is stuttering now.

QUESTION
—What is wrong with Mr. Terupt?

Detective Luke

Jeffrey

It didn't take long for me to get bored at home. Plus I was missing Asher. So I decided to get Mom out and take her to the center.

I didn't bother asking if she wanted to go. I simply told her we needed to go, which was the truth, more or less. It was part of my research.

We walked into the center and Nurse Barry greeted us.

"Hi, Jeffrey," she said. "We haven't seen you in a few days."

"I know," I said. "I've been at home. I brought my mom with me today."

Nurse Barry reached out to shake my mom's hand. "Hi. I'm Nurse Barry. We love having Jeffrey visit. He's great with all the kids, especially Asher."

"I know he loves coming," Mom said. "Thanks for letting him."

"We wouldn't ever say no." Nurse Barry turned to me. "Asher's in his room, Jeffrey. He's probably starting to get hungry again. Would you like to change him and give him his next bottle?"

"Sure," I said.

In the beginning, Asher couldn't take a bottle very well. His suck reflex wasn't strong enough. There was no telling whether that was a result of his being abandoned, but it was one of the reasons he needed the center. He was much better now, though, and I loved feeding him. Mom and I started off toward the back.

"Jeffrey," Nurse Barry called after me.

I turned around to face her. She didn't say anything else at first. Probably because she had something difficult to tell me.

"The police are closing the investigation," she finally said. "They haven't been able to find Asher's parents. He's almost fully recovered, so he'll be ready for a permanent home soon. He'll go to foster care until he's adopted."

I nodded and tried a smile but could only manage a fake one. Asher was healthy again. This was good news, but I felt like I was losing another brother all over again. I wished there was a way for me to keep him forever.

Asher had his own room because he was the only infant at the center. I heard his little jibber-jabbers before we even walked in. His dark brown eyes stared up at us. Mom looked down at him and immediately her hands flew up and covered her mouth. I watched her fingers press against her lips and her eyes soften. I was ready for her to cry, but instead she surprised me by reaching down and picking him up. She rocked Asher in her arms and started humming softly. She carried him over to the changing table, at which point I stood in complete shock. I hadn't seen my mother like this in a long time. She looked peaceful. Mom talked and played with Asher. I got the supplies she needed in order to change him and feed him. I did that without talking because I didn't want to break the spell. Once they settled in the rocking chair I left them alone.

Mom and I were quiet on the way home. I really didn't know what to say. I was afraid of saying the wrong thing and ruining everything that had just happened. After she parked the car in our driveway, Mom turned to me and said, "Thank you for bringing me to the center, Jeffrey." Then she leaned over and kissed me on the top of my head before climbing out.

I sat there thinking—about a lot.

december

LUKE

"Hey, Lukester," Mr. Terupt said. I was sitting at a computer in the lab working on my post–head trauma Power-Point. I was going back over my slides to see if I had any mistakes or if there was anything else I should add. "Your work looks terrific," he said.

"Thanks."

"Seems like you've learned quite a bit."

"Yeah," I said, glancing up at him. "More than I thought I would."

"Why don't we go and have a chat at one of the tables? Save your work and I'll meet you over there."

The computer lab was in the back of the library, so it was easy for us to find a place where we could talk privately. The rest of my class continued working. I knew what Mr. Terupt was going to tell me. "I'm okay. Don't worry." I could hear it coming. But I didn't know if I could believe him—not after all that I had researched. I sat down across from him.

"Luke," he said, placing his hands on the table in front of me, "I can't let you share your presentation."

I couldn't believe it. That wasn't what I expected.

Mr. Terupt leaned closer. "Your PowerPoint looks awesome, but I'm afraid sharing it will do more harm than good. Once you teach everyone else about these brain things, they're going to start worrying—and for no reason."

I scowled. Worrying for no reason? I didn't believe him.

"Luke, I'm fine. You don't need to be concerned," he insisted.

"Then how do you explain the dizziness and stuttering?" I wanted answers. I needed a sound explanation. Scientists like proof.

"It's not uncommon for people to experience those things after head trauma. It's not severe and it won't be permanent. The doctor thinks my minor spells are simple side effects from the medicines I'm taking."

"You've seen a doctor?"

"Yes. I'm taking care of myself, Luke. Don't worry."

I was quiet, mulling over all that he had said. I felt a little better, but I still worried—I couldn't help it.

"I have another idea I hope you'll consider for your Power-Point. It's something extra special and super top-secret."

"What is it?" I said.

"So does that mean you'll keep all that brain trauma information to yourself?"

I didn't say anything. He waited.

"You're okay?" I said.

"I'm okay."

"Promise?"

"Promise," he said.

"Okay, I'll do whatever you want."

"Thanks, kiddo. Now here's what I was thinking."

Mr. Terupt leaned closer still and whispered his idea to me. Man, he wasn't kidding. This was definitely extra special and super top-secret. I was big-time excited.

QUESTION
—How can we make our plan work?

Detective Luke

Danielle

After lots of hard work, it was finally here—PowerPoint Presentations Day! The classroom looked terrific. We had spent all morning cleaning, decorating, and arranging so we could share our research in the afternoon. We moved our desks into a big U shape so that Ms. Newberry's fifth graders could sit on the floor—we had invited them. We also needed that space for the cart holding the LCD projector.

The LCD projector is the thing you plug into the computer and then it broadcasts the monitor image wherever you point it. We planned to aim it at the front of the room, where we had the white screen pulled down. Our school owned one LCD projector, which was kept in the library and traveled from room to room on a black cart. Mr. Terupt sent me and Peter to get it.

Getting the equipment was a piece of cake. No need for celebration. But our trip back to the classroom ended with fireworks.

"Here, Danielle. You carry this." Peter handed me the LCD projector. It wasn't heavy, but it was a very expensive item. "Watch this," he said.

The cart was made of hard plastic. It had three shelves, one on top, one in the middle, and one close to the floor, just above the wheels. A side of the top shelf consisted of a strip of outlets with an attached electrical cord. This was so you could plug the cart into a wall outlet and the LCD projector into the cart. When not in use, the cord was wrapped around a couple of hooks.

Peter grabbed on to the sides of the top shelf and placed his feet on the bottom one.

"Peter, what are you going to do? I don't think this is—"

With one foot he pushed off the ground several times like you would on a scooter. He leaned forward and zipped down the hall, heading straight for a declining ramp. Once he got there, Peter picked up speed and sailed straight down. I'll admit, it looked like fun, but on the other end of the building, closer to the annex, there was a much longer and steeper downward slope.

"I don't think you should ride down this ramp, Peter. It's too big. It's not safe," I warned him.

He didn't listen. Anna had told me that Peter didn't like to take advice from girls. It was too bad he didn't learn his lesson the first time he ignored one of us. Instead he got a running start and flew down the hall. And even though Peter traveled at breakneck speed, everything that happened next felt like slow motion.

The black electrical cord slowly uncoiled. The dangling end fell closer and closer to the ground. Then, in a flash, one of the wheels grabbed the plug and swallowed it. The cart slammed to an instant stop and Peter was launched over the top. He hit the ground and rolled right into the person who happened to be coming around the corner at the most perfectly terrible time.

Mrs. Williams had a talent for perfectly terrible timing. The sudden collision knocked her to the ground and her momentum carried her legs up and back over her head. How many kids actually got to see their principal's underwear twice? I had a clear shot right up her skirt. And this time it wasn't innocent flowered underwear. Mrs. Williams needed to go to confession for wearing those things.

I rushed over to help her up. Mrs. Williams brushed herself off and smoothed her clothes. Then she looked at us. "Well, Peter, I'm happy to see you're having fun again." And that was it.

I don't think Mrs. Williams had the heart to discipline Peter. It was still too soon after last winter. Someone else and there would have been consequences. But not Peter. Not yet. He was still healing. I understood, but I wondered how Peter felt about it.

Dear God,

Thank you for not letting anything go terribly wrong with the cart. Crashing into Mrs. Williams was bad, but thank you for not letting anyone get seriously injured. I don't think any of us could deal with another tragedy just yet. Amen.

Peter

Things weren't great. I had this grand plan to fail sixth grade, but the truth was, I didn't think it was going to work. Dad had already scheduled an interview with the admissions office at Riverway without even asking me about it. I'd have to attend that next month. And Mr. T wasn't bothered by my lack of work. My time with him was slipping away, and I felt like I had no control over it. I felt sorry for myself, and because of that I didn't care—about anything. That was why I raced down the halls on that cart ignoring Danielle's pleas to stop, because what did it matter?

I cruised down the baby slope near the library with no problems. It was fun. Danielle tried to stop me from racing down the steep ramp.

Her words just motivated me to go even faster. I took off with a running start. I didn't want what my father wanted.

I didn't want to listen to anyone. Danielle was the one with me in the hall, but my father was the person I pictured in my head. I tore down that ramp until the cord caught in the wheel, then everything slammed to a halt. I catapulted right over the top of the cart.

I found out that Mrs. Williams is one tough woman. I flattened her when I came tumbling down the corridor. The collision was so violent I didn't even realize who I'd crashed into at first. Once I came to a stop, I sat up and the first thing I saw was Mrs. Williams's underwear—again. I only saw them for a second because Mrs. Williams recovered quickly. She just got up and rubbed it off like a professional football player. But I couldn't shake the image of her underwear from my head. They looked like something Lexie would wear. Then I realized Mrs. Williams was staring at my pants. Probably to see if I'd wet myself again. How embarrassing. To her surprise, I could tell by her raised eyebrows, I was dry. She should have checked *my* underwear. What was she going to do to me?

"Well, Peter, I'm happy to see you're having fun again," she said. That was it. Then she walked up the ramp. The only other time I remember being that shocked by a teacher's response was last year when Mr. T told me to tie a knot in my you-know-what after I kept sneaking out to the bathroom.

After the shock wore off, I got to thinking that maybe Mrs. Williams hadn't yelled at me because she felt bad for me. That was not what I needed. If that was how she and Mr. T felt, then they'd never fail me. My plan wasn't going to work. I didn't know what to do.

Jessica

FADE IN: LS of the classroom. We see the desks arranged in a big U shape with the cart holding the LCD projector stationed in the middle. MS. NEWBERRY's class is spread out on the floor while MS. NEWBERRY sits next to MR. TERUPT and MRS. WILLIAMS along the side of the room. MR. TERUPT and LUKE walk to the cart. It's LUKE's turn to present. He is the last to go.

MR. TERUPT

Thank you to Ms. Newberry's class for coming to see our presentations and for being such a terrific audience. I also want to tell my class that you've done a wonderful job. And now for our last presenter—Luke.

MR. TERUPT gives LUKE a high five.

CUT TO: CU of slide #1—THE SCIENCE BEHIND LOVE

LUKE VO

The science behind love.

CUT TO: LS of the classroom. We see LUKE from behind, standing next to the cart. We can see past him to the screen, and we see everyone else sitting around the room, watching his presentation. Some of MS. NEWBERRY's STUDENTS are giggling. They can't handle LUKE's topic. They're not mature enough.

CUT TO: CU of LUKE. He's straight-faced, all business and completely serious about his presentation.

CUT TO: Next slide. We see images that depict the five senses—eyes, ears, nose, lips, and skin.

LUKE VO

Is it all about the five senses? How does he or she look? How does he or she smell? Taste? Feel? Does he sound confident? Does she sound lovely?

CUT TO: MS of various students in the audience. The camera moves from one area to the next, spanning the classroom. We see boys blowing pretend kisses, girls poofing their hair and batting their eyes.

CUT TO: Next slide. We see pictures of various butterflies.

LUKE VO

Male and female butterflies release pheromones in the air to attract mates. Some of these perfumes can be smelled from over a mile away.

CUT TO: Next slide. We see one ugly monkey, a red bird, and a green lizard.

LUKE VO

A very red face for this monkey, the bald uakari, is a sign that he is healthy and likely a good mate. The great frigate bird does not have red feathers, so he pumps a massive amount of air into the red pouch on his throat. Females can see his ballooned-up red throat and are attracted to it. And our green anoles will use color changing to attract a mate.

CUT TO: Next slide. We see a spider.

LUKE VO

And my personal favorite, the Australian redback spider. The male will perform a dance for more than an hour in front of the female he is trying to impress. If he stops too soon, or if he doesn't have the right moves, the larger female will bite his head off.

LUKE's spider story gets a big reaction. We hear exclamations of "Awesome!" "Wicked!" "Eww!" "Whoa!"

CUT TO: Next slide. We see a picture of a man and woman getting married.

LUKE VO

When our senses like what they detect, signals are released in the brain telling us he or she is the one. In the animal kingdom, if all goes well, then a mate is chosen, not eaten. In people, if all goes well with the courtship, then a likely next step is a ring and a proposal.

CUT TO: MS of LUKE as he pulls a small package from his pocket. LUKE walks over to MS. NEWBERRY and hands her the box.

MANY STUDENTS

Oooh!

MS. NEWBERRY smiles at LUKE and tilts her head in a playful gesture. She begins opening the box. She gasps. Slowly, she looks up and MR. TERUPT gets down on his knee in front of her.

MR. TERUPT
(to Ms. Newberry)

Sara, I want nothing more than to spend the rest of my life with you. Will you marry me?

MS. NEWBERRY
(tears in her eyes)

Yes . . . Yes!

THEY embrace.

FADE OUT.

I started crying when Mr. Terupt proposed; many of us did. I thought of Ms. Newberry in the hospital waiting room last year, only wanting a chance to get to know Mr. Terupt better. I was so happy for her. I was so happy for him. Mr. Terupt had fallen again. But this time, he fell in love.

anna

Winter had arrived. It was bitter cold and frost covered the ground most mornings. Lexie stopped riding her bike to school and started taking the bus instead. So I didn't think it was important to tell Mr. Terupt about seeing her bike at the abandoned house. But Lexie kept changing.

It wasn't just lipstick anymore, but eyeliner and bling, too. She called her jewelry "bling." And she had other new words. Things were suddenly "sick" and "nasty," which in her world, meant the best—or in her new words, "the bomb." She thought her outfits were "sick." She thought her "fresh" look was something special. At least, that was the feeling I was starting to get. She had a new attitude with her new everything else. It scared me because I didn't like it. I was beginning to wonder if the old, mean Lexie was on her way back. I hoped not.

Even though we were done with our PowerPoints, Jeffrey and I kept visiting the center. Jeffrey so he could see Asher, and Mom and me because we liked volunteering our time with the patients. After dropping Jeffrey off at home one night, I asked Mom to try that scenic route again. With all of Lexie's changing, I needed to see if she was still hanging around that abandoned house, even though I had no idea what being there meant.

As we neared the house on Old Woods Road, a black car came barreling from the driveway and fishtailed onto the road in front of us. As it sped by in the opposite direction, I caught a glimpse of Lexie in the backseat. She wasn't smiling or laughing. She looked scared.

"Lexie's your friend," Mr. Terupt had reminded me. I didn't know why at the time, but it was clear to me now. A friend's help was what she needed. Mr. Terupt didn't want me to be afraid to tell on her. It was the right thing to do. It was what Lexie needed me to do, and what any good friend would do.

The next day Jeffrey and I sat waiting for Mom after school. We were on our way to the center again. But then the unexpected happened.

"Anna, your mother just called," Mr. Terupt said, hanging up the classroom phone. "She has to stay late at work today so she can't make it."

"Ugh," Jeffrey said.

"Don't worry. Ms. Newberry and I are going to take you guys instead. I've been wanting to see Asher anyway, so now I have the perfect reason."

"Awesome!" Jeffrey cheered. "Terupt and Newberry save the day."

Jeffrey and I climbed into the back of Ms. Newberry's car. She drove while Mr. Terupt rode shotgun. I clicked my seat belt, and that was when it hit me. Here was my chance to be a friend. I knew Jeffrey really wanted to see Asher, but this was a one-time opportunity. I didn't have to tell on Lexie; I was going to bring help to her instead. This was the sneakiest thing I'd ever done. My heart beat faster. My mouth went dry and my hands felt all sweaty.

"Ms. Newberry, could we take the scenic route, if that's okay with you?"

"Sure, that sounds nice," Ms. Newberry said.

Mr. Terupt smiled and Jeffrey gave me a weird look but I didn't say anything. We turned down Old Woods Road and approached the abandoned house.

"That's it," I said, pointing ahead to the place.

"What?" Mr. Terupt asked.

"That's it! Pull over!"

"Anna, what are you talking about?"

"That's where Lexie's been going." I pointed again. "Pull over."

Ms. Newberry stopped on the side of the road in front of the house. What now? I thought. Mr. Terupt leaned over and honked the car horn. Then he got out and yelled.

"Alexia! It's Teach!"

I got out with him. The ground was barely white, but we could see our breath. Mr. Terupt reached in and honked the horn again.

"Alexia!" he yelled.

"Lexie!" I yelled.

She came bursting out the front, jumped off the porch, and ran to Mr. Terupt. She was crying. Sobbing.

"I'm so sorry," she said. She buried her face in his chest and he wrapped his arms around her.

"It's okay," he said. "We're here now."

I felt really bad for Lexie. What had she been doing that had her so upset? I walked over and held her with Mr. Terupt. It was just like last year in Mr. Terupt's hospital room when Lexie went from bad to good. I felt a warmth in my heart with this hug, too, but it didn't last as long because that black car came barreling from around the back of the falling-down house. There were several older-looking kids in the car. The boy driver stuck his middle finger up at Mr. Terupt and then fishtailed onto the road and sped away.

What was Lexie doing with those kids?

Alexia

Gateway drug. That was one thing Peter and Danielle talked about in their PowerPoint presentation. That's like saying smoking cigarettes and drinking alcohol could, like, open a doorway to trying other stuff. Badder stuff. Listening to them present, I wondered why they picked this topic. I didn't realize it had everything to do with me. But Teach did.

I took a drag on my cigarette. I didn't cough. I was getting better at it. I was chillin' on the green couch, hangin' with Lisa and Reena while they did their homework. Brandon had gone out to his car to get something.

Once it turned cold, Brandon started picking me up from home with his car every day. We'd chill for an hour or two at the hangout until it was time for the girls to go to basketball practice. Brandon would give them a ride and then drop me back at home. He had nothing else to do. He said he couldn't handle the sight of his teammates working out on the mats without him, so he stayed away from wrestling. He was messed up over it. I felt really sorry for him.

"Got a treat for you today, kindergartner," Brandon teased, rejoining us in the back room. "This stuff is dirty." He held up a plastic sandwich baggie filled with what looked like dried-up green leaves.

"Dirty" meant "wicked good." Same as "nasty" or "sick."

Suddenly I wasn't chill anymore. I didn't know what that stuff was, and it made me nervous.

"I just scored this bag of weed. I bought it right in school," Brandon bragged. "Stupid teachers. None of them understand what I'm going through."

That slap in the face woke me up. That was the second time Brandon had ragged on his teachers. Like, I felt bad for Brandon, but I didn't believe what he was saying. I had the best teacher in the whole world, and like, I knew he cared.

Then I heard his voice coming from outside. "Alexia! It's Teach!" My heart took off.

"What was that?" Brandon yelled. The girls looked at each other and shrugged.

Then again: "Alexia!"

I had the best teacher in the whole world. He knew and he cared. I flicked my cigarette into the ashtray and ran out of the house. I jumped off the front porch and ran straight into Mr. Terupt's arms.

"I'm so sorry," I said. I cried and cried. It hurt so much to disappoint him. Feeling his arms hold me made it hurt more and less all at the same time. He wasn't giving up on me. I was lucky.

Jeffrey

December was a month I had grown to hate over the last two years. The holiday season always made me miss Michael even more. That wasn't any different this year, but other things were.

All of a sudden Mom and Dad were talking to each other. I found them drinking coffee together at the dining room table one morning, so I made a point to look and see if it was happening again the next day, but instead I found them lying in bed together. I still didn't know what it was, but the holiday season was filling my house.

When I got home from school one afternoon, there was a Christmas tree waiting. We'd had a tree last year, so it wasn't that big a deal, but decorating it together was. Mom played our holiday CDs and we pulled out ornaments that I didn't even remember we had. Then we had a family dinner. All three of us sat down and ate together, a wonderfully decorated and smelling tree in the background.

I did most of the talking, telling them all about school. I told them the story of Luke's presentation, and how Mr. Terupt was going to marry Ms. Newberry.

"Now, that's a proposal I've never heard of before," Dad said.

"How did you propose, Dad?" I asked.

He looked at Mom and smiled. She gave a sheepish grin back.

"When I was a little girl my daddy gave me a music box," Mom said. "It was my favorite thing in the whole world. Your grandfather died when I was in high school, and that music box stopped working shortly after that."

"Your mother told me about it when we were dating, and I never forgot," Dad said. "I made her a new music box and gave it to her one night."

"He had me in tears before I even opened it," Mom said.

"What happened when you did open it?" I asked.

"I found this," she said, showing me the diamond ring on her finger.

Dad reached across the table and took Mom's hand in his. They were smiling, and so was I. I went to bed that night happier than I'd been in a long time, still having no idea that the best was yet to come.

When I walked into the house after school the next day, I found Mom and Dad in the living room. Mom was rocking Asher.

"He's going to be with us for a while," Dad said. "We've become his foster parents."

That was when I started believing in angels.

PART TWO

january

Alexia

Like, there was a lot happening with me in the new year. For starters, I had a job. I was working at the Pines with Mom after school. Mostly I cleaned the dishes, but once in a while I got to wait a table or two, or seat some of the guests. The cook was a guy named Vincent, and boy, could he whip up some delicious foods. He also told the corniest jokes in the world, like, "Why wasn't Cinderella any good at soccer?"

"I don't know," I said.

"Because she always ran away from the ball."

I liked Vincent and his dumb jokes, and I loved being with Mom. The restaurant was a cool gig. It was all thanks to Teach—and Anna.

Teach came and rescued me from the Old Woods hangout. He knew something was up with me, and Anna helped him discover my secret. I still can't believe she had the guts to do that. I mean, part of me is mad that she ratted me out, but I also realize I had gotten myself into a mess that I didn't know how to get out of. I was crazy scared when Brandon pulled out that plastic baggie. I wasn't ready for that. I feel like Anna was my guardian angel. I'm so lucky to have her as my friend and Teach in my life. He wasn't one of those teachers that didn't know or didn't care like Brandon talked about. I sometimes wonder what I'd be like if Teach hadn't shown up. I piled into the backseat of Ms. Newberry's car with Anna and Jeffrey after we watched Brandon demo his infamous fishtail exit—his middle finger included free of charge.

No one said anything in the car. Ms. Newberry drove to a different school, where Anna and Jeffrey got out. They met up with Anna's mother. I figured I was next to get dropped off, but that wasn't the case. Instead of going to my empty house, we ended up at the Pines.

Turns out Teach had been to the restaurant before that day to talk to my mom. His concern for me intensified when Mom was unable to make the parent-teacher conference back in October. Probably not that big a deal under normal circumstances, but I was the only one without a parent to attend for the second year in a row. That was, like, reason enough for Teach to start paying closer attention to me— that and my mysterious "after-school program."

There was a lot of explaining to do, but Teach knew I'd been through enough for one day, so we just ordered dinner and sat and ate—Teach, Ms. Newberry, Mom, and me—together.

The next day Mom surprised me by showing up to give me a ride home after school.

"What're you doing here, Mom?"

"I thought you and I could spend the rest of the day together," she said.

"What? But aren't you working?"

"Not today," Mom said.

I smiled, but like, there was a lot going on in my head. I was glad Mom was there, 'cause I didn't know what I was going to do after school. I mean, I knew I wasn't going back to the hangout, but like, I was confused, too. Why wasn't Mom at work? Did she get fired or something?

We climbed into the car and headed home, but not the normal way. Instead, Mom took us down Old Woods Road. I held my breath.

"That's where you've been hanging out, huh?" Mom said as we drove past the old house.

"Yeah," I said.

"No more," Mom said. She was laying down the law, and I was happy to accept it because I desperately wanted her back in my life. "You understand?"

"Yes, ma'am."

I think that was the first time I ever called Mom "ma'am." I remember thinking I sounded like Danielle. But like, it was serious talk, and I was giving Mom a serious answer. I'm not stupid. I knew Mom had talked to Teach. How else would she have known? But the question was, how much did she know? I think what she found out was how little I knew, 'cause when we got home Mom explained everything to me. Like why she was working so much.

Normally, when two people get a divorce and children are involved, the parent not having custody of the kids pays child support. That means my dad would be sending money to my mom every month to help her pay expenses. But that wasn't the case, so Mom was working long hours to make enough money for us. When I learned that, I started crying.

"I thought it was 'cause you didn't care about me." I rubbed my eyes. "I didn't think you wanted to be with me."

"Of course I want to be with you, Alexia. You're all I have."

Mom wasn't getting any child support from Dad because they weren't divorced. Mom had simply told him to get out, and that was it. She didn't have the money to pay a lawyer for a divorce, plus Dad had threatened her. Told her that if she came looking for any of his money there'd be trouble. Mom started to cry.

I told Mom I wanted to help. "I want to work too," I said. "I want to work at the restaurant with you. Then we can both make money and I can be with you in the afternoons."

That's how I got my first job—and my mom back.

Jeffrey

"Mr. Terupt called," Mom said.

It was after school. I was home with Mom, Dad, and Asher—what was beginning to feel like a family. Things were terrific! Nothing had happened at school, so I didn't know why Terupt would be calling.

"Your father talked to him. Go ask him what it was about," Mom said.

Dad was in the kitchen making dinner. We ate together every night now. Mom and Dad took turns doing the cooking, and I did the cleanup and dishes. Mom stayed out in the living room with Asher. I could hear her singing to him.

"Dad, you talked to Terupt?"

He stood up from the oven, where he was bent over checking the chicken. "Yes." He turned around to wash his hands in the sink. "You and I are going down to the high school after dinner. Mr. Terupt will be there."

"What for?"

"Mr. Terupt thinks . . . and your mother and I think, we ought to give it a try—"

"Give what a try?"

Dad dried his hands on the towel hanging from the refrigerator door. "Wrestling," he said, looking at me.

Suddenly it was quiet. Dad was waiting for my reaction, and Mom wasn't singing. Was she listening from the other room? "Terupt can't wrestle," I said.

"Actually, he said he used to do a lot of it, and that he can tell you'll be good at it."

"He said that? How can he tell?"

"I don't know. But let's at least try it out," Dad said. "Mr. Terupt will be there tonight, helping the head coach, and he's hoping to see you."

So we ate dinner and I cleaned up, and then Dad and I drove over to the high school for my first wrestling practice.

We walked into the gym, where mats were spread all across the floor. There were kids running around on them, and some were already wrestling with one another. I recognized a few faces from school, but most of the kids I didn't know.

"Hey, stud," Terupt greeted us. He must have seen us walk in. "Mr. Mahar," Terupt said, shaking my dad's hand. "I did a lot of wrestling growing up, Jeffrey. You're going to be a natural at it. Plus, it's a great way to get your anger out without getting in trouble." He smiled and jokingly smacked me on the back, but I knew he was being serious. He took me over to the mats.

"Were you good?" I asked him.

"I did all right," Terupt said.

I knew better. There wasn't anything Terupt did where he was only "all right."

The coach blew his whistle and all the kids started jogging in the same direction around the gym. It was time to get started with the warm-up. I joined in. We did some rolls and flips, and then some stretching. Next we learned the double-leg takedown. Terupt came out on the mats and helped me go over the technique. We practiced for a while and then it was time to scrimmage. I was paired up with a kid from a different school.

The only training I'd had before that night was with Dad at home. When I was little Dad and I would horse around. He'd take me down and I'd get out from under him because I couldn't stand how hot it was underneath him.

The coach blew his whistle for us to start and I moved toward my opponent. I kept my hands out so I could stop him if he tried to shoot for my legs. When I got close enough to him I grabbed his head and tried to pull him down. He fought to stand up just the way Terupt had told me he would. I let go of the kid's head and tackled his legs when he straightened up.

That was when I found out Terupt was right. I was good at wrestling.

That was the beginning for me—the night I became a wrestler.

LUKE

Mr. Terupt came back from the holiday break with another unbelievable project idea. I daresay this project was so special and so unbelievable that no other class anywhere has ever tried it. For us, however, it was typical Mr. Terupt.

We rounded up the chairs for a class meeting. The detective in me observed something very much out of the ordinary while we were doing this—Danielle hurried out of the classroom, not even bothering with the girls' pass, which was already in use.

"Okay, gang," Mr. Terupt said. "It's time to get you started on the next major project."

No one interrupted. We sat up straight and listened carefully. We knew that these were always hard-to-believe announcements.

"We've had some pretty awesome projects over the past

year and a half, but this one might be the most important. I'm not going to pass the microphone around this time. I just want to share my idea with you."

"What is it already?" I blurted out, knowing I didn't need the microphone to speak up. Plus, I couldn't take it any longer.

Mr. Terupt chuckled. "Okay, here it is. Ms. Newberry and I have decided to put you guys in charge of planning our wedding."

Whoa! What? I knew weddings were a huge deal, but what exactly needed to be done to make one happen?

The classroom remained silent, so I think everyone was probably thinking the same thing. Finally, I spoke up. "Mr. Terupt, what does that mean? What do we need to do?"

"There's a ton that needs to get accomplished," Mr. Terupt answered. "This is a big task, but Ms. Newberry and I feel confident that you are up to the challenge. Having you guys involved will make it all the more special for us. Many people will tell you it's the most important day of their lives. For Ms. Newberry and me, it will be."

Mr. Terupt paused, letting his words sink in. He rose from his chair and walked to the easel. I noticed him wobbling a little. I didn't like that. Another dizzy spell? I wondered.

Mr. Terupt continued, "Ms. Newberry and I have thought about all that needs to get done, and we thought about what roles would be good for some of you. I've made a list under this chart. If you don't like what we have in mind, let me know, and we'll discuss other options. Those of you without an assigned responsibility will need to think about what you might like to do, or where you might like to help, and then let me know." He flipped the chart.

> **Wedding Date:** June 25, one week after sixth-
> grade graduation
> **Where:** Outside at Snow Hill School
> **Wedding Manager:** LUKE

I didn't even read the entire chart. I stopped once I got to my name. I've always wanted to earn the highest grades and be the best student, but that's always been for me. Suddenly I was presented with a challenge that I *had* to do the best for someone else. For Mr. Terupt *and* Ms. Newberry. Counting blades of grass had been a tough project last year, but this one had it beat. I was excited.

QUESTIONS
—Where is Danielle?
—What does managing a wedding even mean?
—Is Mr. Terupt okay?

Detective Luke

Danielle

"Class meeting," Mr. Terupt announced. I was excited. We were back from our holiday break, and I just knew he had something special planned to kick off the new year. I started to move my chair over to the circle, but then stopped. I could feel it. The girls' pass was already out, but I beelined to the bathroom anyway. Mr. Terupt didn't say anything. I'm sure he sensed something was wrong, because everyone knew class meetings were my favorite.

Once in the bathroom I ducked inside one of the stalls. I fumbled with the button on my pants in a rush to get them down. When I finally got them off, I glanced at my underwear and saw the red stain. I started crying. It was terrible. This was my third time bleeding, my first in school. I was scared. I didn't want anyone to know what was happening to me. I hadn't told a soul. I sat on the toilet and buried my face in my hands and cried. But not for long, because my stall door was suddenly pushed open.

"Are you okay?"

It was Lexie. I didn't even look up.

"Whoa! Like, you've totally got your period!" Lexie sounded thrilled. I took my hands away from my face and looked at her. Then her excitement vanished. Her head lowered and her shoulders slumped. "You're so lucky," she said to the floor.

"*Lucky?!*" I looked down at my underwear. "I'm bleeding. How is that lucky? What does this even mean?" I used my shirtsleeve to wipe my face.

"Every girl's gonna get her period," Lexie said, "but you're the first. You are lucky. When you get your period it means, like, you're a woman . . . not a little girl. Congratulations. I try all these things, pretendin' to be grown up, but you really are."

"Lexie, I don't know what to do. I haven't even told anyone."

"Don't worry," she said. "I'll help you."

"I'm not telling anyone!"

Lexie put her hands on her hips. "Like I said, every girl gets her period. You're just the first in our class. Now c'mon."

I finished in the stall and then followed Lexie back into the classroom. The class meeting was over and everyone was at their desks again, including Mr. Terupt. I wondered what Lexie's plan was. I found out soon enough. She walked right up to Mr. Terupt.

"Teach, Danielle got her period. I'm gonna take her to the nurse."

I couldn't believe it. Lexie just came right out and told him. Thank God she whispered it. I was so embarrassed.

164

Now it wasn't just my down-there that felt warm, but my face did too. And then I saw that Mr. Terupt was blushing.

"Oh. Gee. Yeah. Good idea, Lexie," he said. "You better go to the nurse. This isn't exactly my area of expertise."

Lexie brought me to Mrs. Barton, who took care of me. She gave me some new underwear and this thing called a maxi pad. Then Mrs. Barton taught me all about my period. I'm actually going to get it every month for something like the next forty years. Afterward, I felt better. She also called my mom and told her the news. That helped, too, because now I wouldn't have to tell her. Mrs. Barton also said that I could ask to come and see her anytime during my period, because I guess there are some times that I might not feel so great. According to her, Mr. Terupt would understand. I told Mrs. Barton that he had said this wasn't his area of expertise, and she laughed.

"Well, sweetie, this is no man's area of expertise. In fact, there's a lot about us women that men don't understand. Ever."

Things were better after that. I know I should feel good about what Lexie said. She's not the best at handing out compliments, and I know she tried. Plus, she meant what she said. But the truth is—I'd still take her fake breasts over my bloody underwear any day.

Dear God,

According to Lexie, I'm a woman now. If that's the case, I'm hoping I can find out about the man from our fields. You must think I'm growing up if you sent this period thing my way. What next? Hopefully not too much too fast. Amen.

Alexia

Like, so there I am, in a bathroom stall, when I hear some-one come walking in. Whatever. But then I hear her start crying in the stall next to me. Once I finished I checked to see who it was.

Danielle was sitting on that toilet seat with her pants yanked down and a big red bloodstain on her underwear. Her period! Like, I totally couldn't believe it. Why did she have to be first? I'd been waiting on my period for over a year and still wasn't getting it. Instead Danielle got hers, and I know it's 'cause she's bigger. Bigger girls can get theirs ear-lier. I know that 'cause I read it somewhere. But like, I didn't say it out loud. I used to be mean like that, but not since last year. Danielle's my friend. And she was upset.

Come to find out, Danielle didn't know anything about periods and what they are or how they work. She was really scared. Like, she actually thought she was hurt or that something was wrong with her. I got her calmed down and took care of her—the whole time wishing it was me instead of her.

Someday. It has to happen someday.

Jessica

FADE IN: It's project time. Students are spread out all over the classroom, some working on the floor, some at their desks, some alone, and others with partners. JESSICA works at the classroom computer. We see MR. TERUPT walk over to JESSICA and pull up a chair to confer with her.

MR. TERUPT
So, what are you working on?

JESSICA
Well, I have two important pieces that I'm preparing to write. One is the wedding announcement, and the other is the wedding invitation. I'm going to look up examples of both to get ideas for how to structure mine.

MR. TERUPT
Sounds good. Your excellent planning is impressive, and it's

one of the many reasons you're a strong writer. I can't wait to see what you produce.

JESSICA smiles. MR. TERUPT begins to stand up.

JESSICA

Mr. Terupt . . . wait.

MR. TERUPT sits back down.

JESSICA

I know Ms. Newberry's first name is Sara, and yours is William, but I was wondering if you knew her parents' names. I've noticed that parent names appear on wedding invitations.

MR. TERUPT

A funny thing—names. I can't stand it when people mispronounce Terupt. I hate it when they say "Tr-upt" instead of "Tare-upt." And I really hate it when they make some stupid remark like "Tr-upt, as in interrupt."

LUKE
(while passing by)

If they spent time with us last year, then they'd know it's Terupt, as in dollar word.

MR. TERUPT and JESSICA laugh.

MR. TERUPT

I hope Ms. Newberry is prepared for her new last name.

JESSICA

She doesn't want anyone else's.

MR. TERUPT smiles big.

MR. TERUPT

Her mother's name is Sandra and her father's is Hank.

JESSICA
(eyes on her journal, jotting down info)
And your parents . . . just in case.

JESSICA VO

It took no small amount of courage for me to ask that question. This was my chance to learn more about the man I didn't completely know. More about my Sam Westing.

MR. TERUPT

My mother's name was Natalie and my father's was Owen.

Both JESSICA and MR. TERUPT are quiet, letting the word "was" hang in the air. MR. TERUPT rises and moves on to the next student.

JESSICA VO

No family. Mr. Terupt had no family in the hospital waiting room, or at his bedside. No family pictures surrounding his desk. His mom and dad were no longer alive. When were they taken from him? I wondered.

anna

I was sitting at the computer next to Jessica one day during Writers' Workshop, researching ideas for centerpieces on the guest tables, when she started asking Mr. Terupt about the names of Ms. Newberry's parents. And I was right there when she asked him for the names of his parents. And he answered, "My mother's name was Natalie and my father's was Owen."

I stayed quiet along with Jessica and Mr. Terupt after he spoke those words. Then he stood and moved on to somebody else. Jessica stared at her computer screen for a while before finally speaking. She knew I was eavesdropping, and I'm sure Mr. Terupt knew too. After all, he has always encouraged us to listen in on his nearby writing conferences. He says we can always learn from them.

"His parents are dead," Jessica said matter-of-factly.

I nodded.

"That answers one of my questions about him. Now I know why he was all alone in the hospital. He's got no one else." Jessica and I both stared blankly at our computers while she talked, but she knew I was listening.

"I wonder how old he was when they died," she said. "I can't help it. I want to know more. That's why I want to write the announcement and invitation. I want to know Mr. Terupt."

Jeffrey came over to us then.

"Hey," he said. "I just got done conferencing with Terupt, and he told me to come and talk to you guys about my idea. He thinks it's a good one."

Jessica and I looked at him and shrugged.

"My mom bought a video recorder to take movies of Asher. She wants to capture the special moments on film so they last forever. The *special* moments. So that got me thinking about the wedding."

"We should make a movie of this whole process!" Jessica yelled.

"Exactly," Jeffrey said. "So I asked Terupt and he said he'd buy the video recorder for us, and I thought I could run the camera while you act as the director."

"Yes!" Jessica agreed. "Yes! What a great idea! Let's do it."

Then Jessica looked at me. "Anna, I need a favor. . . ."

So the short story is, I inherited the task of writing the invitations and announcement because I knew what to do after eavesdropping on Jessica's conference. I was fine with that. I got Danielle to help me, and Jeffrey and Jessica started plans for the movie.

Peter

I was already worried that Mr. T wasn't going to fail me, and then he really put a wrinkle in my grand plan with his wedding announcement. I *had* to help with that project. It was for Ms. Newberry and Mr. T. Their wedding was flat-out way too important for me not to get involved. Besides, I knew exactly what I wanted to do. I was going to be the DJ. I had all of Richard's equipment. I'd put on a party they'd never forget.

But even though failing school seemed unlikely, I wasn't giving up. That's why I told the admissions lady at Riverway exactly how I felt. My father had scheduled the tour and interview without asking me. He assumed I'd be going there like all the men in our family before me. But he was wrong.

"I appreciate your time today, but I won't be attending Riverway," I told Ms. Dawson, the admissions lady interviewing me.

"Oh?"

"I can't leave home. I'm sure you hear that a lot, but it's different for me. I've got someone I need to keep an eye on. Someone I need to be there for."

We talked some more and then Ms. Dawson said, "Well, Peter, you seem pretty set in your decision. Tell me, why are you even here?"

"I haven't exactly told my parents yet. I haven't had the chance, and my father scheduled this visit and interview today without ever asking me how I felt about it."

"Oh," she said again. "I see."

"Could you not contact my father about our talk? I'm not ready for him to find out yet."

"We mail out our decision letters in March. He'll find out then, but I won't tell him beforehand," Ms. Dawson said.

"Thank you," I said. We shook hands and I started toward the door.

"Peter?"

I turned around.

"Good luck."

I nodded and left. I had a long and quiet ride home with Miss Catalina, our au pair. I kept asking myself the same question over and over. How was I ever going to tell my father? Maybe I'd start by asking Danielle to put me in touch with God.

february

Jessica

FADE IN: The classroom is bustling with activity. Students are working all over the place but we can tell the organized chaos is normal routine.

JESSICA VO

Readers' Workshop became a time for students to work on either independent reading or wedding work. Naturally, everyone chose to do wedding work despite the fact that Mr. Terupt had given us a wonderful reading assignment.

CUT TO: Days earlier in the classroom. MR. TERUPT stands at the front.

MR. TERUPT

Okay, gang. We've got a lot going on right now, so trying to do another class novel is not the best idea. However, that does not mean we aren't going to be reading. I'm going to ask you to be very independent and responsible for the next few weeks—even more so than usual. You have two major assignments to complete. You'll need to decide which to work on during class time, and which to save for home. One task is obviously your wedding work. The other is a very special journal assignment that goes along with your reading.

JESSICA smiles and sits up straight. What could be better than a reading assignment?

MR. TERUPT
(continued)

One of the best things about reading is when you connect. By connect, I mean something you read allows you to relate to a character or reminds you of something you've experienced. Or what you read might remind you of something else you've read. When you have meaningful connections, you tend to really enjoy what you're reading, and it helps you understand the text at a much deeper level. If you connect with a character, then you'll be able to tell me how that character feels because you'll have felt that way, or if you are reminded of a different story, then you might be able to make smart predictions. For your assignment, I want you to focus on connecting with your chosen book. I want you to write in your journals about the meaningful connections you have. Then pick your best connection and explain how it helps you understand the story at an even deeper level. And if you *really* connect with your story, then you might also be able to tell me how it helps you in your life.

CUT TO: Back to the classroom and Readers' Workshop/ Wedding Workshop. JEFFREY is following behind JESSICA with his video camera in hand. THEY approach PETER, over by the lizard tank.

JESSICA VO

I love reading, but my wedding work was something that had to be done in school. I couldn't very well make a documentary of the wedding process if I didn't film it while it was happening. Peter was going to be our DJ for the reception, but I wanted to ask him if he'd be willing to help me with part of the documentary. After filming, the footage would have to be edited, then music would be added. That was the part I thought Peter could do.

JESSICA

Hi, Peter. Mind giving us an update on your wedding work?

PETER continues to stare into the lizard tank.

JESSICA

Peter, is everything okay?

JEFFREY puts down his camera and leans closer to peer inside the bog.

JEFFREY
(glaring at Peter)

What did you do?!

PETER
(glaring back at Jeffrey)
I didn't do anything! Don't blame me!

JEFFREY
Then what happened?!

PETER
I don't know.

JESSICA
Guys, calm down.

JESSICA holds her hands out like two stop signs, one pointed at JEFFREY and the other at PETER.

PETER
You really think you're something special because Mr. T started you on wrestling, don't you?

PETER pushes past JESSICA's stop-sign hand.

JEFFREY
What are you talking about?

PETER
Don't play dumb with me. I've heard you talking about it. I know you got that pretty mat burn on the side of your head from wrestling with Mr. T. You're his little pet.

JEFFREY

That's what you think? So you killed the lizards?

JEFFREY pushes past JESSICA. PETER plants both his hands on JEFFREY's chest and shoves him. JEFFREY grabs the back of PETER's head and pulls him to the ground.

JESSICA VO

I've been reading *The Outsiders* by S. E. Hinton. It's an older novel, but a very good one. In it there are two groups of teens at war with each other—war with violence and fighting, like Peter and Jeffrey. Cherry is a girl in the novel who befriends boys on each side of the war. She wants to keep the groups from fighting, but feels helpless. That was exactly how I felt watching Peter and Jeffrey tussle on the ground. I wanted them to stop but didn't know what to do. My feeble pleas did nothing, except attract the man who wanted me to write about these sorts of connections. I found out that was the best way for me to help, though.

MR. TERUPT grabs both boys by their scruffs and marches them out into the hall.

FADE OUT.

Peter

"It's time for you to read this," Mr. T said, handing me a book with a red cover. "I know you'll relate to some of it."

The book was *Wringer* by Jerry Spinelli. Mr. T gave it to me after he gave us the making-connections assignment. I held the book, turning it over in my hands, thinking this was my chance *not* to do a major assignment so Mr. T would fail me. But deep down I knew I wasn't failing this year—no matter what. I was upset about that, but even more upset to think about being forced to attend Riverway next year. I looked closer at the cover of the book Mr. T had selected for me. Underneath the title I found the words *Not All Birthdays Are Welcome*. Just like not all school graduations are welcome, I thought. That was the first of my many connections with this great story.

Palmer LaRue was the main character in *Wringer* and

he was someone I understood completely. I shared Palmer's dilemma. I knew exactly how he felt. Palmer felt pressure to be what his father wanted, even though that wasn't anything he desired. And Palmer wasn't able to talk to his father. Boy, did that feel familiar. I really enjoyed reading the book because of my connection with Palmer, and I was glad to see Palmer's situation turn out okay in the end, but my real-life problem was still there after I finished the last page. It left me feeling miserable and short-fused.

The stupid heat lamp for our bog didn't turn off one night. I don't know why, but the result was two overheated and dead lizards. I noticed them during Readers' Workshop when I was returning *Wringer* to the book area. No one paid more attention to those lizards than Jeffrey—not even Luke, and he bought them. Naturally, Jeffrey had a strong emotional reaction to discovering the lizards. He took it out on me because I was the one back there. If it had been Anna, Lexie, Luke, or anyone else standing next to the bog, Jeffrey would have jumped all over them, too. But it was me—short-fused and miserable.

Jeffrey blamed me. He wanted to know what I had done to the lizards, like I had killed them or something. I couldn't stay quiet about his getting to wrestle with Mr. T, about his being the pet, any longer. It went down fast, and before I even realized it, I shoved Jeffrey and then we were on the ground. I grabbed one of his legs and he draped across my back. That was about as far as it got before Mr. T started pulling us apart.

"That's it! Let's go, you two." He grabbed both of us by

our shirt collars and marched us out into the hall. There was a tone in his voice and strength in his grip that made us listen. "What's going on here?" he demanded. "Huh?"

Neither one of us said a word. We kept staring at the ground.

"Peter, I'm going to have to get you to wrestling with Jeffrey so you can get some of your bottled-up energy out—in a more constructive way!"

Jeffrey and I glanced at each other while keeping our heads low. We both smiled once we made eye contact. Then Luke came into the hall.

"Mr. Terupt, I'm sorry to interrupt your conference, but Jackson and Lincoln are dead. It appears the timer malfunctioned and our heat lamp never turned off last night. They were overheated."

Jeffrey mouthed the words "I'm sorry" to me as Luke was telling Mr. T the news. I did the same back. Then we put our arms around each other and walked back into the classroom, leaving Luke and Mr. T in the hall.

Jeffrey

Anniversaries. They come around every year for special events or dates. For anything that you feel the need to remember, even if you wish you could forget it. For me, there was an anniversary this month. One year ago Terupt was dropped by Peter's snowball. I'm sure that's why Peter was on edge. He was remembering that day, too. I should have thought about that before I blamed him for the lizards. But so much was different since that wish-you-could-forget-it day. When you stop to think about it, it's pretty amazing how much can happen and change in the course of a year.

One year ago I was living in a silent house. Now I had a family. A year ago Terupt went from lying in the snow to lying in a coma, and now he was teaching me at wrestling practice. Ms. Newberry went from quiet tears in the hospital waiting room to crying in Terupt's arms after saying yes to his proposal. In a short time there would be another date to mark as an anniversary, and this would be one everyone wanted to remember.

It was decided by all of us, minus Terupt and Ms. Newberry, that a perfect wedding gift would be a bookcase. Hard to argue against that idea when they're both teachers and love books almost as much as Jessica. We also agreed that the gift would be most special if we were the ones to design and build it. That was where I came in.

Dad and I were put in charge of making the bookcase. That decision made good sense too, since my dad already had all the tools we needed. I thought of Mom's music box and wanted to put as much love into making the bookcase as Dad had put into that. One year ago my dad and I never spoke. Now we had a project that put us together in his workshop for hours.

We took all sorts of measurements and made the necessary crosscuts. We ripped and notched some boards. We prepared the wood by giving it a smooth sanding and staining. Then we built the bookcase. Dad made it very sturdy by securing the boards with glue and screws. It could have held an elephant. Last, we took designs that Anna's and Danielle's mothers had sketched. We taped the images to the sides of the bookcase and wood-burned them in. The bookcase came out beautiful.

Working with my dad was great. He taught me a lot, and I liked spending all that time with him. It also gave us the chance to have an important talk one night.

"Jeffrey, your mother and I have been discussing something." Dad stopped staining and looked over at me. I kept my head down and let him keep talking. "After you took your mother to the center, she took me. She wanted me to meet Asher. Right away we knew that we wanted to be the ones to adopt the little guy." Dad put his hand on my shoulder. "You've helped your mother and me see a lot of things. I don't want you to think that we're trying to replace you . . . or Michael. We only have Asher because of you." Dad started to choke up. I heard it in his voice. He turned back to his board.

"I want us to adopt him too," I said. "I've hoped for that all along. I think Michael helped me find Asher. It was a miracle that was supposed to happen."

Dad nodded. "I like that thought," he said.

Working alongside Dad helped the two of us grow closer. The bookcase turned out just the way I had hoped.

Of course, the other thing that helped us get to know each other again was wrestling. Peter thought my wrestling was all about Terupt. While he was my coach, and I did get to spend extra time with him, I never thought about it as being the "teacher's pet" until Peter exploded. When he shoved me I grabbed the back of his head and pulled him down to the ground. If he wanted to blame me for my wrestling then I was going to show him some of my moves. I didn't want to fight Peter. I wasn't going to punch him. Instead, I wrestled him. I stuffed his head under my belly and lay across his back. He had to put his hands on the ground in order to keep his face from running across the carpet, so he couldn't try punching me either. I had him pinned like that until Terupt collared us. Terupt escorted us out into the hall and solved our problem without even knowing it. He suggested Peter also needed to attend wrestling. We left the classroom angry with each other and reentered only moments later as buddies again.

Closer to the end of the day, when I had a chance to talk to Terupt alone, I told him why Peter had exploded and what he had said. I told Terupt that I thought Luke and the other boys also needed to be invited to wrestling so they didn't feel left out. He agreed and said he'd take care of it. We both smiled and chuckled. I wonder if he was laughing about the same thought—Luke wrestling. This was going to be interesting.

anna

Finding dead animals is not a fun thing. I had the sad experience one day back in the fall when I visited Danielle on the farm and we walked the pastures with Charlie. I didn't know what we were looking for, but Danielle and Charlie kept peering off into the distance. Well, we found something, all right. We ended up stumbling upon a newborn calf that hadn't survived the night.

"Aww," I whimpered.

"Probably a stillborn," Charlie said. "Poor mother."

The mama cow was standing near her baby, bellowing. She was nudging the calf with her nose, trying to get it to stand up. I remember thinking about how much that mother wanted her baby and how there was no dad nearby. It was sad.

So now I had a little experience with discovering a dead animal. Luke did not. After Peter and Jeffrey got into their surprise scuffle, and after Mr. Terupt had taken them into the hall, Luke walked over to the tank and found his two lifeless lizards. You could tell he was upset, not crying upset but staring-into-the-tank-and-not-saying-anything upset. The rest of us stayed back and watched him, none of us knowing what to say or do. After a few minutes Luke walked out of the room, and then Peter and Jeffrey came back in all buddy-buddy. That was bizarre, since they had just been in a fight, but it wasn't surprising, because Mr. Terupt knows how to fix things. Next Luke came back in with Mr. Terupt and they walked over to the tank.

"Luke, I'm sorry," Mr. Terupt said, putting his hand on Luke's back. "I'm not sure what happened."

"They were cooked," Luke said.

"I think we should dedicate our morning to honoring Lincoln and Jackson," Mr. Terupt said. "We'll give them a funeral service."

Luke turned and looked at Mr. Terupt. "Okay," he said.

So that was what we did. Mr. Terupt sent me and Danielle to the library for newspapers. The task was a cinch. Without Peter, there weren't any crazy towers or runaway carts. I couldn't even imagine what nutty idea he would have come up with this time. The papers came back intact and ready for use.

Danielle and I passed the newspapers out to our classmates and everyone began working. We used the papers to find example obituaries so we could write our own for Lincoln and Jackson. Jessica was the only exception. She was on the classroom computer searching for obituaries. She was an expert at finding things on the Internet.

"Did you want a paper?" I asked her.

"Oh, no thank you." She sighed. "If I only knew where Mr. Terupt grew up then I could research his past and find more answers."

"We're supposed to be writing obituaries for Lincoln and Jackson," I reminded her.

"Yes, I know," she said. "I thought I could locate his parents' obituaries, but I need to know where they lived."

"I know where he grew up," I said.

Jessica looked at me now, her eyes big and wide. "You do?"

I nodded. "The answer's written on the inside cover of *Belle Prater's Boy*. I saw it when I was moving his books this summer."

"Did you read that one?" Jessica asked.

I nodded again.

"I liked that book," Jessica said. "A boy searching for his disappearing mama, wondering where she could have gone and what possibly could have happened to her. It's natural to wonder . . . and want some answers."

Jessica got up and walked over to the bookshelf. She pulled out *Belle Prater's Boy* and opened it. She smiled.

It's natural to wonder and want some answers. Did Jessica say that to make herself feel better about researching Mr. Terupt, or was she trying to tell me it was okay *for me* to go after answers about my dad? Maybe you could go after answers if you were prepared for whatever the truth might be. Maybe that was why Mom hadn't ever told me about my dad. She didn't think I was ready. If I asked her, she'd let me know if I was ready or not. It was beginning to feel like time.

Jessica

FADE IN: We see JESSICA sitting at the classroom computer. ANNA is standing by her side, leaning over and reading the screen with JESSICA.

JESSICA
(in a low voice, to Anna)

Here it is.

JESSICA and ANNA lean closer to the computer. CU of the screen.

TRAGIC CAR ACCIDENT LEAVES STAR WRESTLER WITH NO PARENTS

By Faith Rikert
March 26

Saturday, March 24, was supposed to be a night William Terupt would remember forever—and for good reason. After dedicating himself to the sport of wrestling for the past four years, Terupt saw his dreams come true when he won the 152-pound state title in a thrilling finals match, thus capping off his perfect senior season (40–0). This was supposed to be what Terupt remembered about that night, but then he lost something more important than his match.

After the tournament's conclusion, proud parents Owen Terupt (William's father) and Natalie Terupt (William's mother) headed home. Unfortunately, they never made it. Around 11:10 p.m. both Owen and Natalie were killed in a horrific car crash. The cause of the accident remains unclear and under investigation, but the one thing we do know is that William Terupt has been left parentless.

CUT TO: JESSICA turns her head to look back at ANNA, and finds MR. TERUPT standing behind them. Neither girl knows how long he's been there.

JESSICA

Mr. Terupt.

JESSICA quickly closes out the computer screen.

MR. TERUPT
(to both girls)
It's okay. I'm not upset. I knew you'd want answers at some
point, and I knew you'd find them one way or another when
you were ready.

JESSICA
(to Mr. Terupt)
You were an only child—like your parents?

MR. TERUPT nods.

ANNA
That's why you were all alone at the hospital?

MR. TERUPT
I wasn't alone. Maybe I didn't have any relatives or family
there, but I had all of you. You don't have to feel sorry for me.
I happen to be a very lucky man.

**JESSICA and ANNA remain quiet. They don't know what
to say.**

MR. TERUPT
Tell you what. Let's have this funeral for our lizards. Then
we'll have a class meeting so you can share what you found,
and so I can explain to all of you what *you've* taught *me*.

FADE OUT.

JESSICA VO

After learning about the secret inside *Belle Prater's Boy*, I sat down at the computer and refined my search. And voila! I found what I was looking for. Not the obituaries for Mr. Terupt's parents, but a newspaper article that explained what happened. It answered a lot for me, but then Mr. Terupt said he'd share with all of us what we'd taught him. That left me with more questions. What could we possibly have taught him? After all, he was the one always teaching us.

Alexia

Part of me couldn't believe we spent the morning worrying about a funeral for those stupid green lizards. I was like, I'm not going to miss them. But the boys were, and some of the girls. So I think Teach decided to make a big deal out of it to help everyone feel better.

It was actually fun. Peter and Jeffrey made a casket out of a tissue box that they covered in craft sticks and decorated. And after digging a hole beneath a tree near our classroom, Luke put Lincoln and Jackson in their coffin. I couldn't believe he touched those things! Then we walked outside in silence, Danielle acting as our pallbearer, which means she was the one to carry the casket. She slowly lowered the casket into the ground. Then we formed two lines, one on each side of the burial site, and we took turns reading our obituaries.

"Lincoln was a leader, like our sixteenth president of the United States of America," Jessica read. "He wasn't afraid to explore new territory in the tank and he hid from no one. Instead he stayed out in the open, where he could see all of us—boy faces and girl faces, young faces and old faces, pretty faces and ugly faces—"

"Peter," I said. I couldn't resist.

"Ha-ha-ha," he said.

There were a lot of smiles around the grave. It felt good to lighten the mood.

Jessica continued, "Like Abraham Lincoln, our anole Lincoln will be remembered for bringing people together. May he rest in peace." She paused, then read her speech about Jackson.

"Never was there a better friend than Jackson," Jessica began. "Much like the way our seventh president of the United States, Andrew Jackson, who looked out for his friends with what became known as the spoils system, Sir Lizard Jackson was always looking out for his friend, Lincoln. President Jackson took care of his friends by giving them jobs, hence spoiling them. Sir Lizard Jackson took care of Lincoln by sharing food with him. One of the best memories we'll keep is the day we watched them share a cricket for lunch. Lincoln had the cricket's head in his mouth, and Jackson had the rear end in his mouth. They each pulled at the same time, ripping their lunch in half."

"Eww!" I said.

The boys laughed, including Teach. I couldn't help it. Those lizards were disgusting. We finished with a quick moment of silence and then went back into the classroom, everyone smiling—even Luke.

So like, I had no issue with Teach taking time to make Luke and Jeffrey feel better about those gross creatures, 'cause he had done something unbelievable for me, too. No, I'm not talking about getting me from the hangout or helping me get hooked up with the restaurant. I'm actually talking about the book he gave me. I really got that connections thing with *Are You There God? It's Me, Margaret*. It was written by some woman named Judy Blume. I read it twice in one weekend. And I'm reading it again!

What is it that Margaret wants? Her period and boobs! How could I not relate to that? I totally understand what it feels like to want those things. Okay, maybe Margaret's a bit clueless, and she has this big religion problem going on, which reminded me more of Danielle, but she also stuffs her bra! With cotton balls! I wanted to tell Margaret that toilet paper worked better. I also wished I could tell her how to kiss. How could she know so much about menstruation but not know how to kiss a boy? That wasn't going to be me! When my time came, I was going to know how to do it. And there's this bigger, more developed girl in the story named Laura, and that's who Margaret wishes she could be. That made me think of Lisa. I was just like Margaret.

I wanted to be like Lisa. I wanted to be Danielle. I wanted my period. I wanted to be Anna, who at least had a boy who liked her. I had worked with Peter to start adding music to Jeffrey and Jessica's movie, and when we started going through the video I noticed that Jeffrey's camera seemed to like Anna the most.

At least our next exchange was coming. I knew how to get the attention of those boys. Things turned out okay for Margaret in the end of her story, so like, that made me brave enough to try again. I was predicting things would turn out okay for me, since I was like Margaret. I hoped.

Danielle

After the funeral service we had a class meeting.

"This is another one of those meetings where I need to do most of the talking," Mr. Terupt said. "Jessica and Anna found an article about my parents while researching obituaries, and so I think it's time I tell all of you about that part of my life. I thought I'd start by sharing one of my favorite connections," he went on. "It comes from Katherine Paterson's book *Bridge to Terabithia*. Just listen to this part about Jesse."

Mr. Terupt read a few sentences aloud. *"He wanted to be the best. Not one of the best. Not second best. But the very best."* He closed the book and looked at us.

"That's how wrestling was for me. My goal was to be the very best, like Jesse, so I woke up extra early every morning to train. My parents saw my sacrifice and commitment and became my biggest fans. My extreme dedication and tireless pursuit of my goal took me to the state championships my senior year of high school. It was the culmination of all my hard work and I wanted my parents there for it. But there was concern about a possible winter storm that weekend and my parents were debating whether to attend. *You can't miss this one*, I told them. I wanted them to see me win."

Mr. Terupt stopped. Physically, he was sitting right in front of us, but I could tell that mentally, he had gone back in time. We stayed quiet. It reminded me of church, when the minister talked about what he had read from the Bible and a serious quiet followed. There was a serious quiet in our classroom now. This was a reading from Mr. Terupt's Book of Life.

"My parents saw me win, but I never saw them again after that," Mr. Terupt continued. "We were walloped by a blizzard that night. One that brought whiteout conditions and fierce winds. Mom and Dad were killed in a car accident on their way home from the tournament."

Mr. Terupt's eyes were moist, but he kept going.

"Fortunately, I was headed to college, which was the best place for me. Wrestling saved my life. The challenge it provided kept me going when I could have easily given up. I have no brothers or sisters, or any other extended family, so I was alone after my parents died. You saw that last year at the hospital. But now I have all of you. Sometimes answers come at unexpected times, in unexpected ways and unexpected places. I never wanted to love again after losing my parents, because losing them hurt too much, but you've helped me change. And you've helped me do something even more difficult than that. Because of all of you, I've been able to forgive myself for what happened."

That was a class meeting that left me with lots to think about. I thought about Mr. Terupt as a boy and all that he suffered, and I thought about what he had said. *Sometimes answers come at unexpected times, in unexpected ways and unexpected places.* I definitely wasn't expecting an answer to my yearlong question about the man in our fields when I got it. Following that class meeting we had to pack up because it was the end of the day. I was folding up the newspaper I had used for example obituaries when something on the front page caught my eye. It took my breath away. I stuffed the paper into my backpack and read the article as soon as I got home and was alone in my bedroom.

LAND WARS

Moonsuc Tribe Sues Several Landowners
By Thomas Freed
November 13

Several rural Connecticut farmers have learned that they are being sued by a group of people said to be descendants of the Moonsuc tribe because the Moonsuc claim the land rightfully belongs to them. They believe the farmers' lands are their tribe's under a treaty signed in the early 1700s. The treaty was an agreement between the United States government and the Moonsuc tribe, giving ownership of the land to the tribe. However, over fifty years later—and this is where it gets tricky—Connecticut was granted state-hood. The Moonsuc argue that the U.S. government never properly bought the land from them, therefore making the land still theirs.

Imagine living and working a piece of land for your whole life, and then suddenly being told it's not yours anymore. And oh, by the way, you're being sued. That's what some rural Connecticut farmers are up against. Good luck finding an easy solution to this one.

The man in our fields must have been an Indian. Excuse me, a Native American. Right now, though, I didn't give two hoots about that sensitive stuff. I was angry! My grandpa and grandma had been living and working this land for a long, long time. My mom grew up on the farm. My dad had been working it alongside my grandparents since before Charlie was born. And now some Indians were deciding it was really theirs, and we actually had to listen. My family takes pride in keeping their word. A handshake is a solemn promise never to be broken. We didn't steal their land, so we weren't giving it back. The Indians needed to fight this treaty thing with somebody else a long time ago. It was too late now. Sorry. I'd pray for them, but I wasn't giving my land back, and neither was my family.

Dear God,

Thanks for leading me to the article, but I'll need your support. I'm not going to say anything to my family, because ignorance is bliss. There's no need for any of them to know I know and then have to worry about me. And they'd worry, especially if they saw me now. I'll be honest, I've been crying all night. I've been crying enough as it is, every time I get my period. Add this new Indian lawsuit on top of that and I won't have a dry eye ever. God, we'll need a way to solve this land war. Please help us with that. Amen.

LUKE

The most important project of my school career was still going strong—my work as wedding manager. So far we were under budget because we had figured out many ways to do things ourselves. Jeffrey and his father were making our special class gift for Mr. Terupt and Ms. Newberry, so we didn't have to buy one. Lexie and her mother and a cook named Vincent were going to prepare the food for the party, so we didn't need to hire a catering company. And Peter was going to DJ the reception, so we didn't have to find anyone else. All this kept our expenses down and allowed Mr. Terupt to spend money elsewhere, like on the fancy video camera that Jeffrey used as videographer with Jessica. Overall, our wedding work was going well.

The only thing I was bummed about was Lincoln and Jackson dying. Losing them was a big blow. They didn't even make it through the year. Yes, I knew they wouldn't live forever, but I didn't expect to be the one to bury them. I was very upset, but I wasn't alone, and I wasn't the one to discover them dead. That had been Peter and Jeffrey, and they got all worked up over it. Their fight wasn't like some dumb girl war that you didn't even know was happening. They took care of it on the spot with a wrestling match in the back of the classroom. I know you're not supposed to fight in school, but this was way better than those crazy girl tactics. Besides, Jeffrey and Peter got over it and made up in no time. The only thing I still don't understand is how their rumble led to me and Peter and some other boys in class attending wrestling practice with Jeffrey and Mr. Terupt. I'm not sure whose brilliant idea that was, but I could have told you from the start that it wasn't a good one.

HYPOTHESIS

If a geek like me participates in a rough and tough sport such as wrestling, it's likely he won't enjoy it very much.

DATA

I walked into the gym and looked over the sea of mats and was hit with a connection. I felt just like Stanley Yelnats. Stanley is the main character in Louis Sachar's book *Holes*. Stanley is sentenced to Camp Green Lake for something he didn't do, same as *I* was sentenced to wrestling practice for something *I* didn't do. Stanley finds that there is no lake at

Camp Green Lake, only sweltering heat and hard work to be done. It didn't take long on those wrestling mats before I was hot and sweaty and tired and looking for an escape.

We did some running and stretching and then practiced techniques. I've always been a fast learner, getting all As, but I surprised myself when I discovered I could learn wrestling moves just as easily. The new move taught that night was a bar arm. It's a pinning move from the top position when you flatten your opponent on his belly and then pull his arms back. This creates an opening under his elbow for you to slide your arm through. You should have your fist in the middle of his back and his arm hooked around your forearm if you've done it correctly. The guy on the bottom can't do a thing. Then you're supposed to push off your feet and try to drive your opponent's shoulder into his ear. This inflicts pain and causes him to roll over onto his back, where you can pin him. I was good at practicing these moves, but when it came time for scrimmaging, it was a different story.

Coach Terupt matched me up with some kid who was around my size, but unfortunately, he wasn't another geek. He had the flashy sneakers, the special knee pads, and some fancy headgear. I knew experience was something that counted as a huge advantage. I had none. My opponent had a ton.

The whistle blew, and seconds later this mat rat had ahold of my legs and took me to the ground. I was on my belly with my arms pulled behind me. He rammed my shoulder into my ear and drove me over onto my back. I thought he was going to rip my arms off. By the time the whistle sounded to signal the end of the first period, I was teary-eyed and in pain. My hypothesis had been tested and confirmed—I wasn't enjoying this. But like all hypotheses, it had to be tested over and over before being accepted as true.

I started the second period on the bottom, again—where I wasn't very confident and didn't know enough moves. It didn't take long for Mr. Mat Rat to flatten me to my belly with my arms yanked back again. This time he not only made my shoulder feel like it was going to come off, but when he had me on my back he wrapped his legs around my head and squeezed. I found out later that this thing with his legs was called a figure four. I thought my head was going to pop like a pimple. I couldn't breathe. I couldn't move. I only got out because the whistle blasted for the end of the second period. There was a God, and he didn't want me to die. But wait . . . there are three periods in a wrestling match.

Fortunately, I started the third period on top. The only thing I knew was that bar arm, so I tried it and I did it my hardest. The last thing I wanted was to let this kid get on top of *me* again. I managed to get him to his belly and I pulled his arm back. That's when I heard his father screaming, "Get up!" But I held him down until the whistle sounded. I couldn't turn him over, but I didn't let him budge. That wasn't good enough for that boy's father. He kept yelling at his kid for not getting away.

I looked over at my dad and saw him sitting against the wall reading a book, something about quantum physics. He had his glasses perched across his nose, and his pocket protector and pens poked up from his shirt. I had a father like

Stanley Yelnats's, and I was so proud of that. I felt sorry for the boy I had wrestled.

CONCLUSION
—Being a geek is in my blood, but I don't think being a wrestler is.

Detective Luke

march

Jeffrey

The next wrestling practice was something Peter and I looked forward to, but not Luke. He decided wrestling wasn't his thing after just one try. It was funny listening to him retell his experience. It was on a day when the three of us sat together at lunch.

· "Hey, Luke," I said. "Peter and I are going to wrestling tonight. Do you want to come?"

Luke shook his head. "No thanks! I need to save my brain and body for the future."

"Maybe you should try it again," Peter said. "You can't be the best at everything your first time."

Luke got excited. "Be the best! I'm never going to be the best at wrestling." He planted his hands on the table and leaned across it. His butt wasn't even in his chair anymore. "Did you see what that kid did to me? He squeezed my head so hard I thought my brain was going to ooze out through my ears!"

A speck of sandwich flew out of Luke's mouth and stuck to Peter's cheek. Luke was so revved up he didn't even notice, and that's saying something for Mr. Detective. Peter wiped the spit and food from his face and elbowed me in the ribs because I was laughing at him.

"Did you *see* what he did to me?!" Luke said again.

"Yes. Yes, we saw it," I said. "He had a figure four on your head."

"Yeah, after he almost ripped my arm off, he put a figure whatever on my head and tried to make it pop like a pimple." Luke sat back down. "No thanks. I won't be going back to wrestling practice." He took another bite of his sandwich. This time it stayed in his mouth.

Peter and I looked at each other and chuckled. Good ol' Lukester. We'd had a feeling wrestling wasn't going to be for him, but we loved it. We went twice a week while Luke stuck to the Boy Scouts. He was working on his first-aid badge now.

Dad and I picked Peter up and gave him a ride to practice one night. Peter and I had been friends all along in class, give or take a few disagreements, but once wrestling became a part of our lives, we became buddies. We were good. Coach Terupt told us we were naturals.

During the scrimmaging there is always a bunch of yelling and shouting from the sidelines. Fathers and even some mothers sit on the edge screaming out encouragement and instruction. Most of the time I don't hear anything. I sort of enter a different world as I'm wrestling and my mind goes blank, and even though it's crazy loud in the gym, everything is silent to me. But that changed one night.

I was in the middle of a match when I heard a series of rapid, sharp clicks. Up to this point, I was undefeated. But when I heard that strange sound, I stopped wrestling, and before I knew it I was on my back. I quickly rolled to my belly and looked up to see what was making the noise. It was a woman. There was no mistaking her.

She stood on the side of the mat holding a piece of mail in her hand. She was all decked out in a business suit and high heels—which explained the clicking sound. She wasn't far from where I lay on the mat, so I heard what she said.

"Your father's in the car. He'd like to know what this is all about. And so would I." She waved the mail in Peter's face, her voice already beginning to rise. She was one mad lady.

The whistle blew, so I was able to get up. I walked over to Peter while all the other kids got ready for the next period.

"What's that?" I said.

"Mind your own business, young man. This doesn't concern you."

"It's from Riverway," Peter said. "Mom and Dad want me to go there starting in seventh grade."

"You mean you aren't coming to school with us next year?"

Peter's mom glared at me, then at Peter. "Peter will be attending Riverway, thank you. There is no choice. It'll be the best thing for him."

"The best thing?" Peter's voice rose. "You don't even know me!"

"That's enough!" she scolded. "Get your things. We're going to the car!"

Coach Terupt must have heard the commotion from across the mats because he joined us. "Hi, Mrs. Jacobs. I'm William Terupt, Peter's teacher and wrestling coach. Why don't we step outside so we don't make a big scene." Too late for that, I thought. Coach Terupt gently placed his hand on Mrs. Jacobs's shoulder and led her toward the exit. On the way out he turned to my dad and asked him to give Peter a lift home.

Ask me how Coach Terupt got that wolverine-lady to submit, and I'll tell you I have no idea. Must have been some virtual wrestling move.

I used to like silent car rides, but this one with Peter was awful. There was so much I wanted to ask and say to him, but I didn't know how. I definitely preferred my rides to the center with Anna. She was easy to talk to, and better-looking too.

LUKE

The whole wrestling experience had me distracted for a few days, so Exchange Day number two snuck up on me. It was here!

I entered the day anxious. I was excited to find out what Mr. Terupt had in store for us, but I was nervous about the unpredictable. As I already mentioned, any hypothesis needs to be tested more than once to be proven true, but I didn't want to run another trial for this one. I expected another fight. I worried about Jeffrey's tolerance and the comments of our soon-to-be-classmates. I hoped I was wrong, which was something I had never wanted before. I hoped it would go better this time—for everyone. I didn't know it, but I should have been worrying more about Lexie than Jeffrey.

Once our guests were settled, Mr. Terupt welcomed them and went on to explain our day's challenge. No stuttering or fights this time—so far so good.

"You'll have the next hour and a half to work as a team. Your challenge is to build a boat that will float, but you may only use the materials provided," Mr. Terupt announced. "Your boat must measure at least one meter by one meter," he continued, "and you should also keep this in mind while building. If more than one craft floats, then we will add weight to each by placing sandbags on them until all but one sinks. The last boat afloat will be the winner."

"Where will we test them?" Tommy asked. I was wondering the same thing.

Mr. Terupt smiled. "We won't be trying to float them today. There's still snow and ice out there. Instead, you will be participating in the first annual Float Your Boat Contest at next month's Snow Hill Carnival."

The mere mention of the carnival brought smiles and cheers from all of us, visitors included. The Snow Hill Carnival came to town once every two years, and it was always one of the best weekends.

"Now that you're all excited about the carnival, let's make sure you have a boat to float," Mr. Terupt reminded us. "Just a few more rules."

He presented all the various items available: plastic bottles, straws, string, Styrofoam, meter sticks, rubber bands, tape, cardboard, and more. The catch was that each item had a price tag, and each group only had one hundred dollars in their imaginary budget. We needed to be smart about how we spent our pretend money. This, of course, was much easier than managing a wedding. I knew I could win this contest. I already had a genius idea for my vessel.

After all the instructions and rules, we were organized

into teams. Then everyone spread out all over the classroom and even into the hall, so we had enough room to build. My group consisted of Lexie and two visiting boys, Derek and Jason. I got them positioned in the corner of the classroom, where I knew we'd have plenty of space. I needed to construct a large boat—one that could support extra weight.

"Have you ever taken a beach ball and forced it under the water?" I asked. "When you let go it jumps out. Why? Because of the air in the ball," I explained. "For the same reason these capped bottles are going to keep our boat afloat."

The boys weren't listening, which was what I was secretly hoping for. And Lexie, well, one look at her and you knew what she was concerned about. She was focused on attracting the two boys. Derek and Jason were totally distracted by her. My group was perfect. I smiled and got to work.

To her credit, Lexie did help by handing me the materials I needed and by holding things in place for me after I got started. Derek and Jason were too busy joking around the whole time, whispering and snickering. I didn't pay any attention to them until we were almost done, and they happened to have what I needed. When I looked over at Derek he had two water bottles stuck under his shirt. They looked like torpedoes coming out of his chest. He was posing for Jason.

"Derek, I need those last two bottles," I said. I wasn't bashful. I was a man on a mission, and my vessel was near perfection.

"Tell you what," Derek said. "I'll give you these bottles if Lexie can give me some of her tissues to blow my nose."

At that, Derek and Jason really started cracking up and

Lexie laughed right along with them. I didn't know what tissues Derek was talking about, and I ran out of patience waiting for my bottles. The only person who looked as agitated as me was Peter. I saw him glaring at my group from across the room. He looked angry.

"Derek, the bottles," I said, holding out my hand.

He reached under his shirt and tossed them to me, but then I needed his help holding things in place because Lexie had disappeared.

In the end, I constructed an interwoven lattice of capped water bottles connected by meter sticks. Our boat was almost as long and wide as I was tall. I had pieces of Styrofoam positioned throughout the middle. This was where the weight would be added. The idea was that by having the bottles of air spread out, we'd have a large enough surface area to keep the vessel and additional weight afloat.

I couldn't wait for the Snow Hill Carnival. The Float Your Boat Contest was going to be intense, but I was feeling confident.

QUESTIONS
—Will my boat win?
—Where is Lexie?
—And what tissues is Derek talking about?

Detective Luke

Alexia

Today was key. It was our second Exchange Day. The first one didn't go exactly as I had planned, so I, like, needed to give it another shot. But I was feeling positive. This time I brought a roll of toilet paper from home. The school TP is one huge roll that doesn't tear easily, and it's very thin. It's impossible to work with. My roll from home was softer and fluffier, and much easier to shape.

Last time I had a few boys eyeing me before Jeffrey went ahead and tackled Derek. And then when things moved to the squid dissection I had boys fighting to get at my table, but the squid smell made me sick and I puked all over the place. Like, how pathetic. At least my stuffed bra gave me toilet paper to wipe my mouth with on my way to the nurse. I was hoping for better results this time around. I might have been done at the hangout, but that didn't mean I was done trying to get boys to look at me.

It wasn't Jessica who found me getting ready in front of the bathroom mirror this time, but the woman in our class—Danielle. "Lexie, what in the world are you— Huh!" she gasped.

"Calm down, Danielle. Everything's okay." I cupped and shaped my chest. "Just think of it as me dressing up," I said. "You know I like to do that." I looked in the mirror and gave myself a final adjustment. As Jessica would say, they looked *abundant*. To me, they looked *perfect*. In the glass, past my reflection, I saw Danielle with her head down in the midst of a prayer. I hoped she was telling God to get busy and help me start developing. I knew God would understand. After all, Margaret had prayed to him about this stuff.

During the exchange, I ended up in a group with Luke and two other boys, Derek and Jason. Luke was a man of science. He didn't miss details, so he noticed me right away. But being a science geek, he didn't pay any attention to my efforts either.

As for the other two boys, one was the kid Jeffrey had tackled, and the other was a wimp. Just my luck. They shot secret glances at me, but neither said a word, and they wouldn't make eye contact.

With nothing else to do, I decided to start helping Luke. Big mistake! Helping meant bending and twisting and reaching to get materials. My first warning came when I turned to grab another water bottle and I felt my boobs shift. Suddenly I had one up by my collarbone and the other closer to my belly button. I froze. I couldn't turn back around and let them see me like this.

"Lexie, do you have that other water bottle?" Luke asked.

I tossed the bottle behind me without spinning around. Then I quickly realigned my chest. I was fast and no one noticed a thing. Or so I hoped. But Derek and Jason started whispering and snickering even more. I knew they were making fun of me—or was I being paranoid? They still weren't making eye contact.

My second warning came when I bent forward to hold something in place for Luke and my left side got flattened against part of our boat. This wasn't a quick fix. I tried a sneaky cup-and-squeeze attempt before sitting up, but I was stuck with a lopsided alien-looking chest. What was I supposed to do? I couldn't run to the bathroom and take them off! That would have been worse.

I tried leaning forward to help Luke again, hoping that would shield my horror. But this time my right side got crunched. This was going from bad to worse, with the worst yet to come. Now I had lumpy and lopsided boobs. I sat up and tried to give myself a quick readjustment, but it was too late. I looked over and saw Derek with two water bottles under his shirt. He was pretending they were breasts. He finally made eye contact with me.

"How do these look, Lexie? They might work better for you."

He and Jason started cracking up. I tried smiling and laughing with them.

Then a clueless Luke spoke up. "Derek, I need those last two bottles."

It wasn't Luke's fault. He was just trying to finish his boat.

"Tell you what," Derek said. "I'll give you these bottles if Lexie will give me some of her tissues to blow my nose."

Then Derek and Jason lost it. They thought they were *sooo* funny. They gave Luke the last two bottles he needed and kept laughing. I didn't know what had happened. I couldn't feel the disaster. The toilet paper under my left side had sprung free and poked up from under my cami. They saw it! A nightmare! I tried laughing along with them again, acting cool, playing it off, but I couldn't keep it up. Luke went back to work and I hurried to get the bathroom pass.

Derek and Jason were jerks. They were about as mean as could be. Having them laugh at me hurt. I can't believe I used to be mean like that to people. I'm lucky to have friends now. They came to my rescue.

Jessica

FADE IN: Camera moves in on LEXIE. She is sitting with her team during Exchange Day number two. She's wearing a pretty cami with a short skirt and black leggings. We see her inflated chest. She has her abundant look again.

JESSICA VO

Looking at Lexie, I'm reminded of someone I'd rather forget. If she changed her top to white, put on fire-engine-red lipstick and nail polish, and kept the big hoop earrings, she'd be Dad's bimbo—the woman he left me and Mom for. I wonder if Dad's bimbo was like Lexie at our age. I don't like these thoughts because I like Lexie.

CUT TO: CU of LEXIE. She throws her head back and laughs up at the ceiling. She bends forward, still laughing, but her hands quickly move to her neck region. CU of LEXIE's hands stuffing something back under her top. Camera pulls back as LEXIE sits up. There isn't anything showing, but we see her wet eyes. LEXIE gets up and hurries out of the classroom.

CUT TO: JESSICA entering the bathroom. We find LEXIE sitting against the wall, her knees pulled close to her chest and her face in her hands. JESSICA sits down next to LEXIE.

JESSICA

I'm sorry, Lexie.

LEXIE is crying. JESSICA wraps an arm around her.

JESSICA

Those boys are evil, Lex. You don't want to bother with them.

LEXIE
(sniffling)

I just want to be good at something. I thought I could be good at getting the boys to like me.

JESSICA

You don't have to try so hard. They're going to like you— everyone does.

LEXIE

If I don't try, they won't even notice me.

JESSICA

Lexie, I know you want the boys to like you, but you want them to like you for who you are, not your you-know-whats. You'll never get any respect that way. You want to be like Ms. Newberry.

JESSICA VO

I sounded like my mother. I was simply repeating what she had told me a long time ago. She claims Dad will realize his mistake someday.

LEXIE pulls some toilet paper from under her shirt and uses it to blow her nose.

LEXIE

You always sound so grown up.

JESSICA

You always *look* so grown up. You're definitely good at dressing to impress. I think you're destined to be great onstage, Lex. You're already a great actress.

LEXIE pulls free more toilet paper and blows her nose again. The GIRLS look at each other and start laughing. DANIELLE enters the bathroom and walks over and sits on LEXIE's other side.

DANIELLE

How are you doing?

                         LEXIE
              (wiping her face with toilet paper)
Better now.

                       DANIELLE
Peter got pretty mad in there watching you work with those
other boys. He must like you.

                         LEXIE
Ewww! Peter! Yuck!

**LEXIE walks over to the trash can and throws out her snotty
tissues. Then she pulls the remaining toilet paper from under her top and tosses that. She turns and faces JESSICA and
DANIELLE. They stand up.**

                         LEXIE
I'm going to Mrs. Barton's for the rest of the day. I'll tell her
I'm not feeling well.

LEXIE gestures to the classroom.

                         LEXIE
I can't go back in there. Not flat as a board.

                        JESSICA
Don't worry. We've got you covered.

                         LEXIE
Thanks.

JESSICA and DANIELLE smile. LEXIE leaves.

FADE OUT.

JESSICA VO

It felt good to help Lexie. That's what friends are for. But what I didn't realize is that Danielle and I had given her reason to start a romance, even though I should have seen it coming.

Danielle

One of the things I've become better at this year is reading people. Just sit back, stay quiet, and watch and listen. What facial expressions is the person making? What gestures or body movements? What sounds, like huffs and puffs or weak sighs? It might sound tricky, but it's not. It's no different from knowing that a snarling dog, his teeth bared and fur standing up on his back, is telling you he's not happy and to get away.

I've been doing this reading-people thing ever since the summer. I knew something big was going on at home, but I didn't know what, so I studied my family members—Grandma and Grandpa mostly.

Did Grandma take time to fold her dish towel or did she throw it down? Did Grandpa talk at dinner or spend most of the time running his hands through his hair and over his face? Did they talk to themselves, as old people sometimes do when they have a lot on their minds?

Since discovering the "Land Wars" article I was the one with plenty to think about. I wasn't as worried about reading everyone else as I was about learning more. I started scanning the headlines every time I found a paper, but I didn't find any new news. The original article was actually from an older newspaper, so I wasn't exactly sure where this land war stood now, and that made me uneasy. Because of this, our second Exchange Day was a welcome distraction.

It was easy for me to read Peter on Exchange Day number two. He was in my boat building group. There were several times when we had to say his name to get him to focus on our work instead of stare over at Lexie. The rest of my group thought he was trying to get ideas on how to build a good boat by looking to see what Luke was doing. While this was a sneaky strategy that made sense, I knew Peter was studying Lexie and those other boys.

That morning, I prayed for Lexie when I found her in the bathroom with all that toilet paper. I had already prayed for me before that. I wasn't very comfortable in my clothes. Nothing fit right anymore. All of my pants were highwaters. A tiny part of me felt better after I found Lexie and saw that I wasn't the only one with clothes not fitting right, but I hoped that wasn't God's way of answering my prayer.

And now I wonder if what happened was God's way of teaching Lexie a lesson. His way of telling her they'd grow when it was time.

Peter's wide eyes turned into a glare every time Lexie

talked to those boys and every time they laughed. Peter got so mad he snapped the piece of Styrofoam he was holding right in half.

"Wha'd you do that for?" Josh, one of the visiting boys in our group, asked.

"I don't know," Peter said. "It was an accident. Here." He tossed the broken pieces into the middle of our materials. "They're making fun of her," he hissed under his breath. "Doesn't she know that?" He was talking to himself and didn't realize I was listening.

Peter was mad that Lexie dared talk to other boys. And once she started flirting with them, Peter got madder than a cow getting milked for the first time. That was easy reading. He was jealous.

Peter didn't see Lexie leave for the bathroom, but Jessica and I did. And it was easy to tell that Lexie was upset. It's too bad Peter didn't notice, because then maybe he would have seen that Lexie hadn't fallen in love with those boys. Maybe then Peter would have calmed down a bit.

In the bathroom, I joined Jessica in trying to make Lexie feel better. But by the time I got there Jessica had already done most of the work. Lexie had finished crying and was beginning to smile. I wanted to be helpful, so I told Lexie about Peter. She acted all grossed out by it, so I don't know how much good I did. I actually felt worse for Peter than I did for Lexie after that.

Dear God,

My friends Lexie and Peter had quite a day today. I'm sure you know all about it. Maybe now Lexie will know to take things slower, but I doubt it. She takes everything too fast. Grandma would tell her, "Patience makes the world go round." Lexie could use a dose of patience. I'm running out of patience myself. Please don't leave me in suspense. I know there's a land war going on, but I don't know how things stand right now. I'd like to know, if you don't mind telling me. Amen.

Peter

Mr. T asked me and Anna to escort our visitors to their bus after Exchange Day number two wrapped up. Even though there were no books involved, Anna and I still made a good team.

We led our visitors to the main entrance and held the glass doors open as they filed out and boarded the yellow bus. Mr. T went outside with Mrs. Stern. They were busy talking. I eyed Derek as he walked past me. He thought he was big and mighty for flirting with Lexie. Anger bubbled inside me.

At some point that afternoon the sky started dropping those big, heavy, very wet snowflakes. The kind you hate to shovel because the snow sticks together and weighs so much. A late-in-the-season snow that melts quickly but is pretty while it lasts. It was snow, though. And that triggered a painful memory and another range of feelings mixed with the anger I already had brewing. For Derek, the snow was an invitation he couldn't resist. He bent down and scooped a handful. I watched him form a snowball. That was all I needed.

I bolted out the door and chased after him. He was about to throw that snowball in Mr. T's direction. I connected with him just as his arm was pulled back. Lowering my head, I tackled Derek, taking him right off his feet. I landed on top of him in the wet grass. I heard the wind leave his body as we bounced off the ground.

You have to imagine how I was feeling. Derek was about to chuck a snowball that could have accidentally hit Mr. T. This had nothing to do with Lexie. It was the first time someone had made a snowball in front of me since last year. My whole body tingled. I was just protecting Mr. T.

"Oh my goodness!" I heard Mrs. Stern shriek.

I jumped off Derek. "You can't throw snowballs here!" I yelled, standing over him.

"You're just mad 'cause I spent the day with your girlfriend," Derek said. He got up and brushed his pants and jacket off.

"She's not my girlfriend," I said. "You just can't throw snowballs here, okay?" I felt other kids gathering around us as Derek stepped closer to me.

"Oh yeah, why not?" he said.

"Because somebody could get hurt," Mr. T said, pushing his way through the crowd and stepping between me and Derek.

"Get on the bus!" Mrs. Stern demanded. "This behavior is unacceptable!" Her class knew to listen. They did as she ordered. "I'll have a talk with them," she told Mr. T. "I'm gonna whip them into shape yet."

Mr. T smiled. "Oh, I know you will, Dolores. I have no doubts about that."

Anna and I started back to the classroom. She knew I was upset over Lexie, so she tried talking to me about it. I changed the subject to Jeffrey. I told her that he had the hots for her, which he did. Anna was taken by surprise. She didn't really get a chance to say anything, because as soon as the yellow bus pulled away, Mr. T hurried to catch up with us.

"Thanks, Peter," Mr. T said. "Everyone should have a guardian angel like you." He put his arm around me.

A guardian angel shouldn't be far away, I thought. Definitely not at Riverway.

"Peter, did you learn how to tackle like that at wrestling?" Anna asked.

"Sort of," I said. "That was a double-leg takedown, except in wrestling you don't get a running start like that."

"Because there's not enough room in the ring?" she asked.

Mr. T and I laughed out loud. "Sort of," I said again. "Except it's not a ring. It's just a mat."

"Oh," she said.

"Did you want to try wrestling, Anna?" Mr. T asked.

I stiffened. I was afraid she might say yes. I couldn't imagine wrestling a girl!

"No!" Anna said. "But I do think I'd like to watch it."

I let out a sigh. Whew.

"Well, guess what?" Mr. T said. "We plan to have wrestling at Field Day this year."

"Really?!" I said.

"Yup."

Awesome! First we had Snow Hill Carnival, then Field Day, then graduation, and then a wedding. This was going to be the best finish ever. The thought of finishing made me wonder—again—what I was going to do without Mr. T next year. All along I'd been telling myself I needed to fail so I could stick around and look out for him, but the truth was I needed him more than he needed me.

My mother is a powerful lady. She's always in charge and people don't question her. But I did that night she showed up at wrestling. I don't know where my courage came from, but I told her how I felt and that I didn't want to go to Riverway. She didn't like that, and was about to lose it when Mr. T stepped in and put an end to our standoff.

I got a lift home from Jeffrey's father while Mr. T stayed back in the parking lot, talking to my parents. It was an unofficial parent-teacher conference. Mom and Dad made it home about thirty minutes after me and then we had a parent-child conference. I was scared.

The mail from Riverway was my acceptance letter, but it came with a condition. It was the condition that sent my parents into orbit and on a rampage to my wrestling practice. I would need to write a letter or revisit and interview again, explaining my change of heart and newfound desire to attend Riverway, before I would be officially admitted. This news came as a surprise to Mom and Dad.

"Peter, do you want to go to Riverway in the fall?" Mom asked.

"No," I said.

Dad got up and left the room. That was the end of my short conversation with him. Mom sighed.

"Okay, Peter. This is too much for your father right now, but I'll talk to him. This letter says we need to wait until after the school year anyway, but if you still don't want to go by then, well, we'll see." Mom got up and walked over to me. She bent down and kissed the top of my head. "Sorry about tonight, honey." Then she left the room.

It was a step in the right direction. My parents finally knew how I felt. Things were still up in the air, and I was nervous about not knowing my future, but after Lexie's performance at Exchange Day number two I almost told my parents that Riverway did sound like a good idea. Except I still needed to be around for Mr. T. I wish I knew the answer.

anna

Peter has a big heart. He would do anything for Mr. T. He was just trying to protect him. By the time I got out there, Peter was already getting off Derek and trying to explain to him that you couldn't throw snowballs here. A crowd gathered around and I started to get very nervous.

"You're just mad 'cause I spent the day with your girlfriend," Derek said.

"She's not my girlfriend."

I heard Peter say that plain as day, but I also heard the defeat in his voice when he said it. I hurt inside to hear Peter sound like that. If he liked Lexie, which he obviously did, then seeing her put a show on for those other boys must have really upset him. But he wasn't the only one that hurt. Deep down, I wanted Peter to like me. I'd had a crush on him ever since the summer. We spent a lot of time together.

"Get on the bus!" Mrs. Stern barked to her students. The crowd that had gathered separated immediately. Everyone listened to her. I was thankful she was there to help, but I was even more thankful that she wasn't my teacher. I would have still been in hiding with a drill sergeant like that. That much I knew for sure.

Peter and I started on our way back to the classroom while the rest of the visitors got on the bus and Mr. Terupt shared a few final words with drill-sergeant lady.

"I'm sorry that what Lexie did today hurt you," I told Peter.

Peter scuffed his foot along the ground. "Yeah, well, whatever. It's okay," he said.

Of course he didn't really mean that, and I wanted to tell him I liked him, but I didn't have the nerve. Peter said something else instead. And when he did, I almost died.

"Jeffrey's got the hots for you, though."

"What are you talking about?" I said.

"It's true. He does. Lexie and I are beginning to edit and add music to the wedding documentary that he and Jessica have been making, and Jeffrey's camera seems to always find you. We need to keep deleting those parts—sorry."

"Well, it doesn't mean anything just because I show up on his camera."

"Maybe not," Peter said. "But when I teased him about it at wrestling practice one night he didn't deny it. He likes you, Anna."

Now I thought something was wrong with me. Two seconds ago I was hurting inside because the boy I liked, Peter, liked another girl—Lexie. But finding out that Jeffrey thought I was special suddenly changed things. Jeffrey had a big heart. And he was cute.

I was upset with myself because my feelings changed so easily, but Mom put me at ease when we had our talk and she said that at my age feelings tended to change like the wind.

She told me this at the beginning of a conversation that had been waiting to happen for so long. We were on our way home from the center. My project with Jeffrey was long over, but Mom and I weren't ready to stop visiting. We'd grown very attached to some of the residents and Nurse Rose, and went there at least once or twice a week.

Since Jeffrey's family had adopted Asher, it was only Mom and I in the car. Sometimes our car rides were silent because we were both tired from busy days, or we were thinking. Other times we had conversation for the whole ride, talking about whatever was on our minds. Mom liked to talk about Charlie, and I never tired of listening to her happy voice. But on this particular day our ride home started out in silence and remained that way until I finally found the courage to bring it up. "Mom, it's time," I said. "I want you to tell me about my father."

Silent riding again. Mom needed a minute to think about what I had said. "Why now?" she asked.

"Because things in school have got me thinking about him."

Mom nodded. "Sounds like a fair enough reason," she said.

"There's more."

"Oh."

"I've noticed how Lexie and her mom are tight with

money, and I know Jessica's mom has money, but what about us? How do we have enough to live comfortably?"

"You're right, honey. You're ready for some answers," Mom said. She leaned over and turned the radio off, then sat back up and took a big breath. "Okay," she said. "You know that Danielle's family frowned upon us because having a child out of wedlock was a situation they couldn't accept. They're very serious churchgoers."

"Yes," I said. "I know."

"But I told you that my parents and I were also very active in the same church."

"I remember."

"Well, sometimes churches organize retreats. Getaways with a spiritual focus. They can be for families, adults, or young people. I especially liked the ones for young people."

Mom glanced over at me. I was following, and had a feeling I knew where she was headed with her story.

"You're probably guessing that I met your father on one of those retreats."

I nodded.

"Well, I did."

I looked at her now. Her eyes stared straight ahead at the road. Me, on the other hand—I went bug-eyed. Two young people making a baby during a church retreat. As Danielle would say, *Holy cow!*

Mom slowed for a stop sign. "We actually saw each other on several retreats before anything intimate happened. He was the first boy to show any interest in me. Naturally, because of that my heart raced whenever he was around."

Mom looked both ways, then eased forward.

"At that young age, your feelings change like the wind when you find out someone likes you," Mom said.

I thought of Peter and Jeffrey. Boy, did Mom have that right. My feelings changed like the flip of a switch. I felt better knowing that was normal at my age.

"This boy was very sweet to me, Anna. He didn't pressure me. He didn't need to. I went along with everything because I liked his attention."

Mom stopped talking and looked over at me.

"Okay, so then what happened?" I said.

"The hard part," my mom answered. "I told your father I was pregnant the next time I saw him, which was at another retreat about two months later. I guess at that point he acted like a high school boy. He was scared and wanted nothing more to do with me. He told me he was sorry. He didn't want to be a dad."

"That's it?" I said. "He just walked away from you?"

"That's it," Mom said. "That was the last time I saw him."

"I thought you said he was a good man." I felt my voice getting louder and the blood pounding in my temples. "He was nothing but a jerk."

"I still think he was a good person, Anna. He just wasn't ready to deal with . . . a pregnancy. He was kind and nice to me. He didn't make me do anything I didn't want to."

"But he left you when you needed him most."

"I let him."

"Why?" I said.

"I don't know. I just did. If he didn't want to be a part

of what was going to happen, then I wasn't going to make him. I would have been dealing with an ugly person—and his family. I didn't want warring families. That would have been too much. I feel better thinking of your father as a good person."

I shifted in my seat and tried to calm myself. We were quiet for a minute before Mom spoke again.

"Are you ready for the rest?" she said.

I sighed, still not happy, but I nodded. How much worse could it get?

"I didn't tell my parents I was pregnant right away. A girl can be sneaky and hide that sort of thing if she wants. I've heard stories of people not knowing a girl was pregnant until she goes into labor and delivers the baby. That wasn't me. I didn't tell right away because I was scared, but I didn't try to hide it once I started showing either. I loved you from the very beginning and was never going to be ashamed of you. Your grandparents didn't handle it well, though, so I never told them who the father was. I didn't see any good coming out of it. My parents were ashamed and wanted me to put you up for adoption." Mom looked over at me. "And then I was met by an angel."

Now I looked sideways at Mom. What was she talking about?

"That's right, an angel," she said.

I nodded, but with my eyebrows scrunched. Mom drove along at a Sunday driver's pace, neither of us in any hurry. There was no need to rush a conversation that had been waiting since my birth.

"Miss Leila Mae was a lifelong friend of *my* grandmother's. She was a sweet old woman living all alone. Well, she heard about what was going on—people talk in small towns—and she came and found me. Miss Leila Mae insisted that if my grandmother had still been around, she would have helped me. Since Grandma wasn't around, Miss Leila Mae took it upon herself to help us."

I tried picturing Miss Leila Mae. I thought of her as a short, plump woman with wavy white hair. I bet she smelled of pie, too. And she probably liked to touch you when she talked to you.

Mom continued, "I started staying with Miss Leila Mae before you were even born. I slowly moved all my things over to her place. Maybe if your grandparents had seen you—just once—things would be different. Babies can change people. They can make miracles happen because babies *are* miracles. Just look what Asher did for Jeffrey's family.

"We stayed with Miss Leila Mae for the next two years. She helped care for you while I completed my GED. When I say I have a GED, people automatically think I must be stupid. But really it was just the result of our situation. The classes were a piece of cake for me and I breezed through all of it. I was actually a very strong student in school.

"During this time my parents sold the house and moved south. Some of the money from the sale arrived in the mail one day. I'm still thankful for that, but that was the end of the help and communication from your grandparents. I haven't talked to them since."

I sat still, staring out the window as we drove down the

road. The air felt thick and heavy around me. And it felt like my heart was beating harder and slower. I was listening to the story of my beginning.

"Anna, Leila Mae couldn't have children of her own, so she thought of us as the children she never got to have. I thought of her as our guardian angel. I have no idea what would have become of us if it weren't for her."

"What happened to her?" I asked.

"Miss Leila Mae passed away just after your second birthday. She died in her sleep one night. In her will she left us her house and all her money."

"Do you mean the house we live in used to be Leila Mae's home?"

"Yes," Mom said.

Wow! I thought. Miss Leila Mae did sound like an angel. We drove past the old airport, site of the Snow Hill Carnival that everyone was beginning to talk about. It was a highlight for our entire community. Seeing it made me think of Danielle and her family. They were among the leaders behind the carnival and were already beginning to work hard to organize and prepare for it.

"What about Charlie?" I said.

"He knows."

I scooched up in my seat, shocked. "What do you mean he knows?" I said, looking at Mom again.

"He knows everything. Like you, he wondered about money and how we were managing. He wasn't trying to be nosy. He was asking out of concern, and wanted to help if he could."

Mom paused while she slowed down and turned onto our road. "The money from Leila Mae and from your grand-parents allowed me to stay home with you until you started school. In those early years I was lucky—I only had to worry about being your mom. We were able to spend a lot of time together."

Lucky, I thought. How many people on the outside thought of us as lucky? Mom was right, though. I felt lucky. I have for a long time. I have the best mom.

"Charlie says we've renewed his faith. He thinks our story is what the Lord is all about. He thinks we know more about faith than most people who go to church every Sun-day. He says his family, except for Grandma Evelyn and Grandpa Alfred, has learned to forgive because of us. Maybe that's part of what the Lord intended."

Mom pulled into our driveway. I looked at our house and wondered if Miss Leila Mae was inside, waiting for us. *Thank you, Leila Mae. Thank you.*

april

Danielle

The Snow Hill Carnival comes to town every two years. It takes place at the old Snow Hill Airport. The airport hasn't operated for a few decades, but it's the perfect place for a carnival because it's one gigantic flat piece of land that can fit all the carnival equipment plus a parking lot. At the back of the field is a hill that leads up to another smaller plot of land where you find Snow Hill Pond, site of this year's first annual Float Your Boat Contest.

The Snow Hill Carnival wasn't a big deal just for our school, but for the whole community. It was a big deal for my family. In some ways, I think it could have been better named a fair, but when it first came to Snow Hill long ago, it came as a carnival. It had changed a lot over the years—now many local businesses participated by running concession stands, and there were church-related and farm-related tents and all sorts of contests—but the carnival title has stuck.

My family got involved in many ways. Dad and Charlie worked with other farmers to prepare the site. They had to mow the fields and clear away any debris that might have accumulated since the last carnival. They helped to set up all the signs and ropes and Porta-Potties. They were there to assist the carnival people when they arrived. Grandpa always said the getting-ready part was way more work than the rest of it. He'd spend a month getting ready and the carnival would be here and gone in two days.

When it did finally start, my family kept just as busy. Grandma and Mom organized all sorts of baking and flower contests. And Grandpa, Dad, and Charlie took care of the cow shows and horse pulls. Grandma and Mom judged the contests, and Grandpa served as the announcer for the horse pulls. The horse pulls were the main attraction on the second night. The first night was always packed just because it was the opening.

The weather had Grandma and Grandpa stressing more than usual this time around. Stressing about the weather was normal for any farmer, but usually it was because of the crops, not a carnival. It had been raining more than normal for most of April, though. And everybody was getting nervous that this year's carnival would be rained out. We did a lot of praying leading up to the event, and it paid off, because the skies cleared for opening night. The parking area became a muddy mess because the ground was still soggy, but that didn't matter.

The only bad part was I had my period again. This was my fourth time. I was still getting used to the whole thing. I had gotten cramps in March and was desperately hoping to skip those this month. I usually got grouchy, too, which Mom told me was normal. I was thinking the carnival would help me forget about my period and everything to do with it.

LUKE

The Snow Hill Carnival was such a big deal that we only had a half day of school that Friday—opening day. All Snow Hill businesses closed early. Everyone in our community looked forward to the event, and by three o'clock, there was a population density at the carnival that made you feel like you were in a major city.

Our Float Your Boat Contest was scheduled to begin at four o'clock. Portable stadium lights lit up Snow Hill Pond and the parking field below us. The water in the pond was much higher than normal because of all the rain we'd had, but that didn't matter for our competition.

We stood in our groups next to our vessels. Each boat had a piece of bailing twine tethered to it so it could be pulled back to shore after being tested. Mr. Terupt wore a pair of chest waders so he could get right in the pond and guide our boats away from shore and into the deeper water. Each group was assigned a number designating the order in which we'd attempt to float our creations. We were number eleven, the last ones—an advantage I liked. More community spectators than I ever imagined joined us for this first-ever contest. When it was finally time to get started, Mrs. Williams unveiled a megaphone for announcements.

"Boat number one!" she hollered.

That was Ben's group. Mr. Terupt guided their boat into the deeper water and gave it a push. It dove straight to the bottom. They had built a submarine!

"Boat number two!" Mrs. Williams yelled. It sank.

"Boat number three!" Her voice hadn't lost any enthusiasm. This one floated like a rock, sinking the fastest of all. There were murmurs among the crowd and doubtful faces all around the pond, but I was optimistic for boat number four. It belonged to Theo, the smartest kid in Mrs. Stern's class.

"Boat number four!" Mrs. Williams called out.

Mr. Terupt gave Theo's creation a shove.

"Hey, it floats!" someone from the crowd yelled.

"Congratulations!" Mrs. Williams yelled.

Enthusiastic cheering and applauding echoed from the hill. That was followed by boats number five through ten, which all found the bottom of the pond like the first three.

"Boat number eleven!" Mrs. Williams announced. "Our final group."

Mr. Terupt nudged our boat away from shore and we watched it float to the end of our twine. Thunderous clapping and whooping rang from the hill. Everyone in our group bumped fists, even Lexie and Derek. There was no fooling around. We all wanted to win. It was us and Theo. Time to add the weight.

Theo had the unfortunate luck of going first. Farmer Wilson took a fifty-pound bag of sand and settled that on the center of Theo's boat.

"One-two-three," Mrs. Williams counted. Then Mr. Terupt shoved Theo's boat back out. Mrs. Williams started her stopwatch, timing how long the boat stayed afloat. After nine seconds the exterior bottles were beginning to lift off the surface and stick into the air. I knew this was because the middle was sinking. It was just like the way the *Titanic* had an entire end lift up out of the water before it went under. At the twelve-second mark Theo's boat was disappearing. By fifteen seconds it was submerged.

"Let's hear it for boat number four," Mrs. Williams shouted. A chorus of hoots and hollers followed, but I was busy thinking. My boat was destined for the same fate unless I came up with something fast. Mr. Terupt and Mrs. Stern pulled my boat over. Farmer Wilson slung the bag of sand over his shoulder and walked toward us.

"Wait," I said. "That bag's fifty pounds, so if we float something heavier, we'll still win, right?" Our teachers and Mrs. Williams all looked at each other, then shrugged in agreement. "Okay. You can put that down," I said to Farmer Wilson. "Peter, I need your help." I asked Peter because he seemed like the right size, and because I knew he liked daredevil stunts. I also knew this was his chance to impress

Lexie. Peter came over, not knowing what I had planned. I whispered my idea to him, and he nodded.

"Why not?" he said. Peter walked over to my boat and lay down on it, face-up. He had his arms and legs spread wide, which I promised would keep him from sinking. His butt rested in the middle, where the bag of sand would have gone. We shoved him out into the water.

After thirty seconds of successful floating and no signs of sinking, my group was declared victorious. We started pulling Peter to shore. Why hadn't Mrs. Williams shouted for us over the megaphone? I wondered. When I looked over at her I found out why.

Mrs. Williams had put her megaphone down and had picked up a nice-sized rock. She smirked and tossed her rock into the pond. It landed right next to our boat, scaring the bejeepers out of Peter, who had his eyes closed and never saw it coming. He yelled and jumped and tipped the boat. Over he went. The hill didn't ring with applause after our victory, but with roaring laughter. The kind of laughing that made your belly hurt.

Peter scrambled to shore and climbed out of the water. Mrs. Williams met him and offered him her hand. "Now we're even," she said. Peter smiled. Then he smiled even bigger when Lexie gave him a towel and celebratory hug.

Our group was presented as the first-ever Float Your Boat Contest winners. Each of our schools had a brand-new plaque to be displayed that would list the names of the victors year after year. Ours would be the first names ever added. That felt pretty cool. In addition to the plaque, Mrs.

Williams also announced that each member of the winning group had earned a pass granting us free rides at the carnival for the night. Awesome! It was also what I had promised to give Peter if he agreed to help me by lying down on my boat. Definitely one of my better bribes.

After the awards presentation everyone scattered. It was time for the carnival. Mr. Terupt, Mrs. Stern, and Mrs. Williams stood together at the edge of Snow Hill Pond looking pleased. It was the first time I'd ever seen a happy expression on Mrs. Stern's face. The first-ever exchange program got off to a rough start with Jeffrey's fists, but there was plenty to smile about in the end.

QUESTION
—Will the rest of my night be as memorable as winning that contest?

Detective Luke

Peter

Mrs. Williams got me good. I was flat on my back, floating on Luke's boat, helping my good buddy out. I had my eyes shut tight the entire time, begging the boat to stay upright. That's why I didn't see it coming when Mrs. Williams tossed a rock my way. The splash was bad enough, but it scared the snot out of me. I jumped and the boat tipped. I leaned the opposite way as fast and hard as I could, which was a big mistake. The whole thing flipped right over and I went under.

Of course everyone thought it was hilarious. Jessica couldn't stop laughing. At least she didn't let out one of those rotten girl farts like Lexie did back in the summer. I made my way back to shore, where Mrs. Williams was waiting for me. I was completely soaked. I was expecting to hear her say "I'm sorry." But instead she said, "Now we're even."

I shivered and smiled. Guess she wasn't feeling bad for

me anymore. I felt lucky and upset all at the same time. Lucky because I knew I had the best teacher in the world and lucky because I knew Mrs. Williams had to be the best principal you could hope for too. And upset because I'd be graduating and moving on in a couple months.

Luke celebrated his victory with the other dudes in his group, but Lexie came over to me with a towel.

"Thanks, Peter," she said. She gave me a big hug in my soaking wet clothes. "You're the hero," she whispered in my ear. When she let go and stepped back, I didn't know what to say.

During the awards presentation I ran to change behind one of the tents. I wasn't going in any Porta-Potties. Those things are nasty. Mrs. Williams had brought extra clothes from school, just in case. When I made it back, the ceremony was wrapping up.

Derek and Jason and Lexie found me. Derek stuck his hand out. "Sorry about the whole snowball thing," he said. "Mrs. Stern filled us in on what we didn't know."

I shook his hand and nodded. "We're cool," I told him.

Derek turned to Lexie next. "I've been wondering all afternoon. What happened to your—"

"I decided you aren't worth the bother," Lexie cut him off. "Besides, I'm interested in someone else." Straight-faced, Lexie didn't flinch. She grabbed my hand and off we went. Time for the carnival. I hadn't even been on a ride and I'd already lost my breath.

Jessica

FADE IN: Aerial view of the Snow Hill Carnival. We see the vast field adjacent to the carnival where hundreds of cars are parked. Headlights are still turning into the lot and driving down muddy paths between the rows of vehicles, looking for places to park. Towering portable stadium lights have been brought in to illuminate the parking area and the pond that rests up over the hill next to the field. They shine brightly now as dusk settles in. It is Friday evening—opening night of the carnival—and virtually everyone from Snow Hill School is in attendance. The aerial view spans over the carnival and we see the bright, rainbow-colored flashing lights advertising the typical carnival attractions. There's a plethora of food tents, everything from fried dough, cotton candy, and snow cones to pizza and burgers. There are games of every sort: water pistols, darts, ring tosses, and more. And then there's the midway. The aerial view zooms in on some of the main attractions. We see the Ferris wheel, the Tilt-A-Whirl, and the long line that has already formed for the roller coaster, the Torpedo.

JESSICA VO

The Snow Hill Carnival is not an amusement park—far from it. The roller coaster (which is always my favorite) tells it all. At an amusement park you get the upside-down, backwards, loop-the-loop, super-fast coasters. Here at the carnival you get the old iron clunker that just races you around the tracks. The Torpedo isn't even outfitted with chest harnesses. The only thing required to hold you in is a metal lap bar that you pull down over your thighs and share with the person sitting next to you. However, despite the less than top-notch rides and attractions, the Snow Hill Carnival has more energy and excitement than any amusement park I've ever visited. I've been told the carnival is the biggest thing that happens in Snow Hill every two years, and now I believe it. The place is full of people I know—my entire class, including Mr. Terupt and Ms. Newberry (though technically she's not from my class), and everyone else from school. There are our exchange partners, as well as all the people from the community and beyond who I don't know. The place is packed!

Jeffrey

The Snow Hill Carnival was all fun and games. I had a blast walking around with my friends. There was a mixture of smells from a million different foods, lights flashed everywhere, and people were screaming all over the place. Jessica couldn't wait to hit the rides. All she could talk about was the roller coaster. She did her best to hurry us through the game area, but we got slowed down.

"Hey, hey, step right up. You're next. Win a prize for your girl over there."

The guy was talking to me, and he pointed toward Anna when he said "your girl." We were walking by the game area when he started heckling me.

"C'mon, Jeffrey. Go for it," Peter egged me on. "Win a prize for *your girl*."

I was embarrassed, but I saw Anna turning even redder. Was that because she liked me too?

"C'mon, you can do it," the man encouraged me.

I handed him my money and took the baseball from him. It was a game where you have to knock the three bottles off the table with one throw. I wound up and fired a fastball. I figured if I was going to miss, I might as well miss throwing hard. The bottles exploded off the table. I hit them with bull's-eye accuracy.

"We've got a winner!" the man shouted.

"Yeah! Woo-hoo!" Peter and Luke smacked me on the back.

"Pick any prize, young lady," the man said to Anna. "He won it for you."

Anna chose a stuffed black Lab. "Thanks," she whispered to me once we started walking again. I saw Peter holding Lexie's hand and thought about trying to hold Anna's, but I didn't have the nerve. How in the world did Peter manage it? Here I was wishing I could be like him, holding a girl's hand, and he must have been wishing he was like me, winning a prize for *his* girl, 'cause he was the next one to try a game. But poor Peter ended up having to climb a ladder and ring the bell at the top. Jessica tried to warn him against it.

"Don't do it, Peter. It's impossible."

"He's not going to listen to you, Jessica. You're a girl," Danielle said.

She was right. Jessica's warning was only more reason for Peter to try it. The ladder was made of rope and it was barely inclined, so it was more like walking a tightrope than climbing anything. As soon as you put too much weight in one spot, the ladder would flip over and you'd fall onto the mat below it.

Peter tried and tried and tried. And we laughed and laughed and laughed.

"Told you so," Jessica said.

Peter was so mad he paid for me and Luke to give it a shot. He needed us to see how hard that thing was. We tried and we failed, but that didn't make Peter feel better. He kept going. He would have blown all his money if Lexie hadn't pulled him away.

"C'mon. Let's go and do something else," she insisted.

Luke didn't want to be left out, so he was next to try a game, but he was smart about it—no surprise there. There weren't any carnival games that called for a battle of wits, so he chose the ducks.

"There's always a winner," Luke announced, pointing to the sign. "According to statistics, this is a good one for me to play."

He walked over and stood next to a large tub full of floating rubber duckies. There must have been fifty or sixty of them—all yellow, all small, all identical. The game was simple: Grab a duck and turn it over to see what number is on the bottom. The number tells you what prize you've won.

Luke reached into the tub and picked one. He flipped it over and found a star on the bottom. This was the most unlikely duck to pick. There was only one with a star and Luke found it. Lucky duck. He won the best prize, a big stuffed yellow Lab that he gave to Jessica.

"I still owe you for the *Westing Game* prize," he said, handing her the Lab.

What was going on?! If Luke ended up holding Jessica's

hand then I was definitely going to grab Anna's. There was no way that little dork was gonna pull that off before me.

"C'mon. Let's hit some rides," Peter said.

We all liked that idea, but Jessica needed to use a bathroom first.

"You guys have made me wait so long, I need to pee now," she said.

She must have had to go bad, because the Porta-Potties were gross. You could smell them from the outside. They reeked! There were at least ten of the blue units lined up at one end of the carnival. Jessica pulled one of the doors open, then quickly shut it and moved on to the next. She went in. That was when Peter decided he would get her back for being right about the rope ladder.

"Miss Told-You-So," he whispered to me. "I'll show her."

Peter placed his hands on the outside of Jessica's Porta-Potty and started pushing on it. I saw what he was trying to do. The thing was too heavy for Peter to shake on his own. This was going to be funny and he needed some help, so I grabbed Luke and pulled him over. Once we started pushing on it with Peter, we got that baby rockin'.

"Hey!" Jessica yelled from inside. We started laughing but kept rockin'. "Hey!" she yelled again. "Stop!"

She started sounding upset, so we stopped. She came out a couple seconds later, and Peter was ready for her.

"We know you like the rides, so we thought we'd give you one you've never been on."

"Funny," she said.

"Oh, calm down. It's not like you pee standing up.

There's no risk of you spraying all over yourself," Peter said. I knew what he was talking about. He was the master of bathroom pranks.

"Eww!" Lexie said. "You're gross."

Peter smiled and we headed off for the rides.

"Hey, where's the stuffed dog I won you?" Luke asked a few seconds later.

"It fell in," Jessica said. She shrugged and gave Luke a sheepish grin. "Sorry."

"That poor dog," Peter said. "He's stuck swimming in the poopy water."

"Eww!" Lexie said again. "You're so gross." This time she elbowed him.

We all cracked up. That was how it went for most of the night—food, games, lots of laughs, and rides—until we had a run-in with some of Lexie's old friends.

Alexia

Mom had to work, but she was going to pick me up at the Snow Hill Carnival after she got off. In the meantime, I spent the night chillin' with my friends—with Peter.

There's always tons of people at the carnival, so like, you can go the whole night without running into someone you know. I wish that's what happened with me, but it didn't. Instead, I ran into the someones I didn't want to see. It happened at the midway. A group of us had just gotten off the Salt and Pepper Shaker, and we were laughing when I heard, "Hey, Little Brat."

I tried to pretend I didn't hear her. I kept walking, a little faster.

"I said, hey, Little Brat." Reena pushed me on the back of my shoulder. I couldn't ignore her now. I stopped and turned around.

"Hi, Reena," I said. "You're looking hot." I was going to try the being-nice approach. I looked over her shoulder and saw Brandon with his head tipped back, drinking from his water bottle. He was walking toward us with Lisa holding his other hand.

"Back to being a kindergartner, huh," Reena said.

I felt my friends move closer around me. "Yeah," I said.

"Look who's here!" Brandon barked. He knocked Reena aside and left Lisa standing behind. He hadn't seen me at first, but once he laid eyes on me he got right up close. "The cops have been nosin' around our hangout. You know anything 'bout that?" he said, his face getting closer to mine.

"She doesn't know anything," Jessica said. "Please leave us alone."

"Shut up, Miss Proper! No one asked you."

When Brandon, Reena, and Lisa first pressured me to smoke back at their hangout, I was all alone. For the first time, I didn't know how to be quick on my feet. So I ended up taking the cigarette and I found myself in a mess after that. Now, surrounded by my friends, I found the courage to stand up to Brandon.

"I don't know what you're talking about," I said, holding my ground.

"Brandon, c'mon. Let's go." Lisa tried tugging him away. She looked at me. If eyes could say *I'm sorry,* hers did.

"Get off me," Brandon said, shaking his hand free from hers.

"How's your finger?" The voice from behind startled me, but once I realized it was Teach, I felt safe.

"Still works, Dent-Head," Brandon said, and he stuck his middle finger in Teach's face again. Then he spun around and disappeared into the crowd. So did Lisa and Reena.

"I'll keep an eye on them," a new voice said. It was Officer Stoneley and he was talking to Teach. Must be Brandon saw him coming and decided it was time to split.

Teach nodded, then squatted down to talk to us. "Nice job sticking together," Teach said. "I'm proud of you guys."

"Thanks, Teach," I said. "Brandon's just upset because he missed out on wrestling season. He got hurt in football."

"He's a wrestler, huh?"

I could tell Teach was busy thinking. I should have said something about Brandon's water bottle. I knew what was in it, especially after seeing how rough and tough he was acting. His short temper told it all. But I had too many thoughts swimming around in my head after that run-in.

"Ms. Newberry, where'd you get that polar bear?" Peter asked suspiciously, nodding toward the huge white stuffed animal she had her arms wrapped around. I hadn't even noticed it.

"I won it for her," Teach said. "Just had to climb a ladder for it."

The boys' jaws almost touched the ground.

"How'd you do it?" Luke needed to know.

Teach smiled. "It's all about physics. And now if you'll excuse us, Ms. Newberry and I are on our way to the car to put her prize away so we don't have to carry it around all night. Stick together," he reminded us.

We did stick together, but the fun had been sucked out

of everything. I stood below the Torpedo with my mind racing faster than the roller coaster. Luke, Jessica, and Jeffrey were on the ride again, but Peter stayed with me. I'd been having a blast, but now I kept thinking about Lisa. What was she doing with Brandon? Why didn't she get rid of him? She reminded me of Mom, and Brandon of my dad. I knew it wasn't easy to get out of those situations. She looked scared. She needed help. Then I thought of Brandon's black car. He would definitely drive like a madman tonight. He needed to be stopped before someone got hurt.

Peter

Wow! What a night! Things were going great! I was hanging with all my friends *and* Lexie was suddenly my girl. We held hands all night long walking around the carnival. We ate pizza and french fries, which Lexie loaded up with so much salt I was sure she would die of a heart attack. She kept shaking and shaking and shaking the container over her basket, and the little white crystals kept falling and falling and falling.

"What? I like salt on my fries," she said, after she saw my twisted face.

"I couldn't tell," I said.

After the fries, I bought her a snow cone—a blue one—and then we cruised around through the different games. After Jeffrey won Anna that black Lab I *had* to win Lexie a prize. That's what a guy is supposed to do for his girl at a carnival.

I should have tried throwing darts or making a basket, but instead I picked the stupid rope ladder. I would have stopped after one try, but Jessica had to tell me *not* to do it, so then I *had* to do it. I blew almost all my money on that dumb thing. If you did manage to ring the bell you won the biggest stuffed animal of the whole carnival—a gigantic polar bear. I really wanted to do that for Lexie, but it wasn't happening. And Lexie knew it. Thankfully, she yanked me away from there before I went nuts.

Before we hit the midway I gave Jessica a free Porta-Potty ride, but she wasn't very appreciative. It was definitely one of my all-time best bathroom pranks. Jessica screamed louder from that than she did for any of the carnival rides, including the Torpedo.

Finally, we hit the real midway rides. We got off the Salt and Pepper Shaker, all of us still laughing as we walked away, and the next thing I knew we were standing face to face with some older kids.

"It's Middle-Finger Boy," Jeffrey whispered to me. I didn't know what he was talking about.

Middle-Finger Boy got right up close on Lexie and I got scared that I was going to have to double-leg him, even though Mr. T had talked to us about self-control. He was messin' with my girl. Lucky for that kid, Mr. T showed up.

"How's your finger?" Mr. T asked. Obviously, he recognized the kid too.

"Still works, Dent-Head," he smart-mouthed back. Then Middle-Finger Boy lived up to his name by sticking his middle finger in Mr. T's face before disappearing into the carnival crowd, along with his girlfriends.

Mr. T bent down to tell us he was proud of the way we had stuck together, and that was when I saw Ms. Newberry holding that gigantic polar bear. Was there anything Mr. T couldn't do?

"It's all about physics," he said.

Mr. T walked away holding his girl's hand, with the massive stuffed animal in his other arm. Luke stood there shaking his head. "Physics," he mumbled.

Danielle and Anna went for some food after that, and the rest of us headed for the Torpedo. But Lexie just wasn't the same after seeing Middle-Finger Boy. And then all of a sudden, she yanked my hand and said, "C'mon." I had no idea where she was taking me, but I felt her determination. I didn't dare say no to her.

She led me past the food tents and past the Porta-Potties and out toward the parked cars before I said, "Lex, where are you taking me?" I had to hurry just to keep up with her.

"We need to stop Brandon," she said.

"Brandon? Who's Brandon?"

She stuck her middle finger up at me.

"Oh. Him," I said. I jogged a few paces to catch up to her. "And how exactly are we supposed to stop Brandon?"

"We need to do something to his car. He's gonna try driving like a macho man out of here, and he's been drinking. Somebody could get hurt. We need to stop him."

"He's been drinking? How do you know that?"

Lexie stopped and turned to face me. "Look," she said. "I just know, okay? Stop worrying about that and start thinking about what we can do to his car so it won't run."

"I know what to do," I said. "C'mon."

We knelt down behind Brandon's car and scooped up globs of mud. It was a good thing it had been raining. The mud worked perfectly. We took the globs and stuffed them into the exhaust pipe.

"It's just like wrestling," I told Lexie. "If you squeeze all the air out of your opponent, then he slows down and stops moving. Mr. T taught me that. The mud's going to choke the car so it can't breathe, then it will stall."

"Are you sure?" Lexie said.

"No, but it sounds good and I don't have any other ideas."

Suddenly Lexie leaned into my body and kissed me—out of nowhere! I think you're supposed to close your eyes when you kiss, but mine stayed wide open. Lexie pressed her lips against mine and all I could taste was salt. Then I started to think it was better that she tasted like salt and not like her legendary fart. Just thinking of that fart made me smell it again. All this was going through my mind while we kissed! And I had no idea what was supposed to happen next. That didn't matter, though, because as soon as Lexie opened her eyes, she spotted Brandon walking toward us from across the parking field.

"Oh no! Here he comes!" Lexie whisper-shouted. "C'mon." We scurried out of sight behind a nearby parked car.

Mr. Macho Man and his girls climbed into the black car. Just backing out of his parking space, Brandon managed to send mud flying everywhere. Once he was in the open field, he stomped on the gas. You could hear it. The engine revved and revved and then began to choke. His precious car jerked along. Steam billowed from his exhaust and the motor made all sorts of terrifying noises as he continued to mash the accelerator. Then all of a sudden, there was a huge bang and the mud shot out of his tailpipe. The engine got the air it needed and the car took off. Brandon wasn't ready and he lost control. He crashed into several parked vehicles. Officer Stoneley was on the scene before they even got out of the car. No one was hurt.

Lexie and I split. The last thing we wanted was for Brandon to spot us. We hurried back to the midway, running hand in hand. But once we got past the Porta-Potties and back to the carnival, we stopped. There was a mob of people gathered around something.

anna

I loved the stuffed dog that Jeffrey won me. I really did, but it made me nervous. I saw Lexie holding Peter's hand and I wanted to hold Jeffrey's—but I couldn't. I was scared to like a boy. I didn't want him to hurt me like my father did my mom. Mom plays it off like she handled it fine, but I know better. I don't want to hurt like that—not ever. I don't think Jeffrey would ever do that on purpose—his heart is too big—but you never know.

After the standoff with Lexie's old high school girlfriends and that terrible boy, I was happy to go and get something to eat with Danielle. I was hungry, and I needed a break from all the rides. I needed a break from everything. We sat down with a couple of burgers under one of the tents.

I wasn't sure what happened or what Danielle heard while we were eating, but she wasn't the same after that. I mean, it was opening night of the Snow Hill Carnival, we were running out of time, and Danielle just said "I don't care" to everything I asked her.

"Do you want to go on the Salt and Pepper Shaker one last time?"

"I don't care," she said.

"Do you want to go on the Superslide one last time?"

"I don't care."

"What's wrong?"

"Nothing."

Obviously something was wrong. Maybe it's her period again, I thought. The rides were about to shut down anyway, so I told myself, There's always tomorrow night. I finally asked Danielle if she wanted to go home. She didn't say "I don't care" this time. She said, "Okay."

We started looking for Mom and Charlie and found a ring of people instead. There was something going on in the middle that I couldn't see.

Danielle

I still hadn't told anyone at home that I knew about the Native Americans wanting our land. I looked through the newspapers every day, and even watched the news when I could, but I hadn't heard or seen anything more about it. I hoped the whole thing was going away, but how wrong I was. Anna and I were under one of the food tents when I heard some of the other farmers talking.

"It's only a matter of time 'fore they're out there walkin' 'cross our fields," one of the men said.

"They'll be lucky if I don't fire my twelve-gauge at 'em if I see 'em on my land," said another one.

"Take it easy, Earl. We don't need another war," said a third man. "Let the courts handle it. It'll work out."

"What's the matter, Danielle?" Anna asked.

"Nothing," I said. "You finished? Let's go."

We got up and threw our plates in the trash. This land treaty thing was still a big problem, and that meant a big worry for my family. I tried to forget about it, but I couldn't. I kept thinking about what the farmers had said. Believe it or not, I just wanted to go home, and it wasn't because of my period. Anna knew it too.

We started looking for Charlie and Terri, but we found a commotion of people instead. I had no idea what the fuss was about.

LUKE

After the confrontation with Lexie's old friends, our group scattered in different directions. I wasn't sure where everyone went, but Jeffrey and Jessica and I headed back to the rides. Jessica was right—this was the best part of the carnival.

It didn't take long for us to make our way to the Torpedo again. This was going to be our fifth time on the roller coaster. What better way to end the night but on the main attraction?

As we waited in line, we watched people who were finishing their ride screaming away. That's why I saw Mr. Terupt and Ms. Newberry get off the roller coaster as we were getting on. And I saw something else that I had missed before—the warning sign. I hadn't seen it until now because the dumb thing was leaning almost all the way to the ground. The paint was chipping off it and you could barely make out the words, but I was able to read the important parts.

Do *NOT* Ride If You:
- **Have a significant physical ailment or condition**
- **Have a bad neck or back problems**
- **Have high blood pressure, heart trouble, or a nervous disorder . . .**

A nervous disorder. That was the part that scared me. Your brain is part of your central nervous system. Why was Mr. Terupt riding the Torpedo? He was at risk. Then it hit me. Why had Mr. Terupt's dizzy spells and stuttering stopped? Was it because he was all better or because he had stopped taking the medications? If he had stopped the medicines, then wasn't he at a bigger risk for a seizure, especially after being jerked around on the Torpedo?

When we got seated on the roller coaster they announced it was the last run. We were lucky to get on again, but suddenly I felt unlucky because I wanted to get off. A sense of doom fell over me. I needed to check on Mr. Terupt.

Jessica pulled the lap bar down and looked at me. She saw I wasn't excited.

"What's wrong, Luke?"

"Mr. Terupt shouldn't have been on this ride," I said. "Not with his brain injury."

Jessica's face went pale. The Torpedo didn't come close to scaring her as much as my words did.

Suddenly, the chain of cars lurched forward. First we banked hard to the left, then we went up a little rise. Once the Torpedo cleared the crest it picked up speed and never slowed down. We took a series of sharp turns at light speed before being shot out of a dark tunnel. People I know who have visited Disney World and ridden Space Mountain tell me that the Torpedo whips you around in the same fashion, just not with all the special effects or for as long—unless you happen to be on the last run of the night. Our operator didn't disappoint. He let us whip around a few extra minutes, and for the first time ever, I was begging him to stop.

It was after we came out of the dark tunnel on our second lap that I saw the commotion. There was a crowd gathered nearby, all huddled around the ground. I started yelling for them to stop the ride. But everybody was screaming. No one heard me. We kept going.

Jessica

FADE IN: The Torpedo comes to a halt and LUKE and JES-SICA ram the lap bar up and jump out of their car. JEFFREY hurries behind them.

                    JEFFREY
              (chasing after his friends)
    Hey, where are you guys going? What's wrong?

                     LUKE
              (running and pointing)
        It's Mr. Terupt.

CUT TO: The sea of people. They're eerily quiet. We can't see past them. We can't make out who or what they're gathered around. We can't tell what they're watching that has them

**mesmerized. LUKE, JEFFREY, and JESSICA fight their way
through the crowd.**

JESSICA VO

I can't see. Let me through! I can't see! Please don't let it be
Mr. Terupt. Not again.

LUKE

I knew he wasn't okay. He shouldn't have been on that ride!

Jeffrey

I was angry. Mad at the world. My life was finally going good and then this had to happen—again! It wasn't fair! Why?!

Peter

There were people everywhere. I couldn't see. I dropped Lexie's hand and tried wiggling my way through the crowd. Someone was on the ground.

Alexia

Teach and Luke knelt next to the body. It was a woman. But who?

anna

"Call nine-one-one!" someone shouted.

"Hang on, Evelyn. Help is on the way!"

My heart almost stopped. My breath was taken from me. It was Danielle's grandma!

Danielle

Not Grandma. You can't take her.

Peter

Once I pushed my way through the crowd and saw what was going on, my mind went back to that day in the snow when Mr. T was the one lying on the ground—unresponsive. Danielle knelt by him and gently slid her hat and coat underneath his head. Luke was also by his side, checking for breathing and a pulse. Jeffrey came running back outside. "Help is on the way," he yelled. Anna was nearby, on her knees, crying silently, with Jessica in hysterics next to her. Jessica was screaming and crying, "Mr. Terupt! No! No!" Lexie and I both stood back watching—alone.

As my mind replayed that snowy day, I heard Jessica's yelling all over again. And then I suddenly realized the frantic cries were for real, except now they came from Danielle.

"Grandma! No! No!" Danielle had pushed her way through the crowd to discover that her grandmother was the one on the ground. She dropped to her knees and fell to pieces.

Anna was right there with her, like she had been with Jessica last year. She wrapped her arm around Danielle. Mr. T and Luke knelt by Danielle's grandma. Jessica and Ms. Newberry stood nearby. I stayed back—frozen in place. I didn't know what to do other than watch. And I didn't even like doing that, but it was another one of those times when you couldn't just turn away. Luke, on the other hand, knew how to respond.

Practice might make perfect for some things, like wrestling, for example. I know I keep getting better every time I drill a move. But there are other things where no matter how much you practice, if you don't have "it," then you're never going to.

I'd been through this scene with Mr. T, Asher, and now Danielle's grandma, and I could tell you I wasn't getting any better with experience. I didn't have what it took in these moments, but Luke did.

"Evelyn, can you hear me?" Mr. T called over her.

No response.

"Evelyn, are you okay?"

Still no response.

Then I saw Luke doing his thing. He held his ear close to her chest and pressed two fingers against her neck. Our Boy Scout with his First Aid Badge wasn't such a dork anymore.

"There's no pulse," Luke said. "We need to start CPR."

Mr. T opened Grandma Evelyn's mouth and made sure her airway was clear. Then he started pushing on her chest.

"Grandma! No!" Danielle cried. "Fight! Fight!"

Mr. T kept going until Jeffrey showed up. "Excuse us. Watch out, please. We're here to help," Jeffrey called out. The crowd parted so Jeffrey could easily get through, along with the two EMTs he'd found at the first-aid station.

There was always a first-aid station at the carnival. Usually, the responders dealt with a few little kids getting skinned knees, nothing more. One year, when it was unusually hot, they helped someone who got dehydrated, but that was the most challenging situation the carnival had ever needed to handle. The EMTs weren't paramedics, just regular citizens, a man and a woman who volunteered.

Jeffrey stepped aside when he reached Grandma Evelyn so the EMTs had room. The guy carried this black case. Luke told me later on that it was an AED, which stands for Automated External Defibrillator. It's like a computer device that tells what to do to an unconscious person and it has those pads that can shock you. The woman carried your classic orange first-aid kit. This was where it got interesting.

"Grandma! No!" the man cried. He dropped the black case and fell to his knees.

"Charlie!" Danielle sobbed.

The man twisted around. "What happened?" He looked at Danielle, desperate for an answer.

"I don't know."

"Where's Grandpa and Mom and Dad?" Charlie said.

"I don't know."

"Mom!" Anna called out. She rushed over to the woman. "It's okay, honey. We're going to help. Stay back."

I couldn't believe it, what were the chances—the man EMT was Danielle's brother and the woman EMT was Anna's mom. Charlie didn't handle finding his grandmother on the ground any better than Danielle. I couldn't blame him. So Anna's mom took over. She never lost focus.

"Do you have a pulse?" she asked Mr. T.

"Not yet." He kept pushing.

"Open the AED," Luke said, pointing to the black case. "It'll tell us what to do. I've used one at Boy Scouts before."

Anna's mom opened the case.

"APPLY PADS," the robot voice from the case instructed.

Anna's mom pulled these sticky pads out of the case. Mr. T stopped CPR and ripped Grandma Evelyn's shirt open. At least she had a bra on! At least it was plain white and nothing crazy like Mrs. Williams's underwear. But then Anna's mom cut the bra right in half. I thought they were going to need to hook the AED to me next. I almost passed out.

They attached the sticky pads to Grandma Evelyn's skin.

"ANALYZING HEART RHYTHM. DO NOT TOUCH THE PATIENT."

The crowd grew very still, all of us waiting to hear what the robot voice would say next.

"SHOCK ADVISED."

The crowd gasped.

"STAY CLEAR."

A surge of electricity was sent to Grandma Evelyn's body, causing her to jump and twitch.

"Grandma!" Danielle yelled.

"ANALYZING HEART RHYTHM."

We were back to holding our breaths and each other. I held Lexie, but not in one of those boyfriend-girlfriend embraces. Any romance we had that night was long gone. This was a hug between two scared friends—nothing more. Then I felt someone else's touch on the back of my shoulder. It was my dad.

"PULSE REESTABLISHED."

Suddenly there were small smiles and sighs of relief. I could tell that everyone felt hopeful. I did. And I felt it in Dad's squeeze too.

Seconds later the ambulance arrived. It tore across the field, throwing mud everywhere. Real paramedics quickly loaded Danielle's grandma into the back, the black case still attached to her. Then the ambulance threw more mud from its tires as it sped away.

The gathered crowd started moving in all different directions again. Lexie spotted her mother and ran to her, leaving me with my father. Everyone else was gone. Dad wrapped his arm around me as we walked to the car. Would he have put his arm around me last year if he'd been with me on that snowy day? I could have used him then. But he was with me now. Things had changed. This was the first time I could ever remember my father showing me any kind of affection. I wouldn't forget it.

may

Danielle

Sometimes when you look back on things it all makes sense. I remember the night before the carnival started. My family gathered in Grandma's kitchen sipping tea and drinking coffee. We had just come home from the carnival site after making sure everything was ready to go.

Grandpa sat in his chair, stressing. I figured he was tired and worried about the carnival, but after listening to those men under the burger tent, I realized he was agonizing over the Indians as much as anything else. Grandma did her best to take care of Grandpa by waiting on him hand and foot—all the while stressing more than he was. And she tended to Charlie and Dad. Like Grandma, we all worried about Grandpa. We should have noticed that all of Grandma's fretting was wearing her down. It was the reason she had a heart attack on opening night.

I'm still not ready to talk about what happened at the carnival. I just can't. Maybe someday I'll be able to, but not yet. I can tell you about what happened after the ambulance left, though.

I rode to the hospital with Dad and Grandpa while Mom rode with Grandma. Anna rode with Charlie and Terri. I remember Dad driving faster than usual on the back roads, and I remember Grandpa staring out his window. I try to imagine how Grandpa must have felt, but I'm not sure I can. I had only known Grandma for a small amount of time compared to Grandpa, and I felt like my world was falling apart.

At the hospital, Grandma was rushed into emergency surgery and I found the waiting room—again. Of course the rest of my family was with me. Grandpa sat staring at the wall, while Dad and Charlie stood off to the side talking in hushed voices. I heard Charlie say something to Dad about the other farmers. Mom joined them, whispering about how it would surely take a toll on Grandpa next.

"I know the Indians want our land," I exploded.

Everyone turned to look at me.

"I said I know those Indians want our land. You don't need to be so secretive around me."

Then the one thing I didn't want to happen did. I started bawling like a baby. I'd been crying over Grandma already, but now I really lost it.

"Get ahold of yourself, Danielle," Grandpa said. Anna put her arm around me. "Your crying won't help anything," he went on. "And it just shows why we didn't tell you."

That made me mad and got me to stop carrying on. I could handle it.

"Those greedy self-entitlin' Indians are after all our lands," Grandpa said to whoever was listening. "They've been walkin' in other fields and devilin' up who knows what sorts of plans. They can't be trusted, that's for sure."

"Grandpa, you shouldn't let the other farmers get you so riled up," Charlie said. "It doesn't do you any good. The courts will handle it."

"You're probably right," Grandpa said, "but if somebody doesn't get riled up, then I fear nobody's gonna stop them Indians."

I woke with a start several hours later. The doctor tending to Grandma entered the waiting room. We all took deep breaths and held them, bracing ourselves for the news he had come to deliver. The doctor pulled the mask off his face and walked over to our family. I kept waiting for one of those big sighs from him, but it never came.

"I think she's going to make it," he said.

We let out huge sighs of relief.

"She's in intensive care and will need about another week in the hospital for us to monitor her progress, but then I expect she'll be ready to go home."

"Oh, thank you, Doctor . . . ?" Mom said.

"Dr. Takoda," he said.

Mom's face twisted at the funny name.

"It's Native American and means 'friend to everyone,'" the doctor said, explaining his name. "That seems like a good thing for any doctor," he added with a laugh.

"Yes. Yes, it does," Mom said. The rest of us were as quiet as when Dr. Takoda first walked in. He was Native American.

Didn't that just complicate our feelings. Was that the trade? Give me my grandma and we'll give you our land?

Dear God,

Thank you for not taking Grandma. We need her. I wonder, did she meet you up there and tell you she wasn't ready? It's wise of you to listen to her. You better just wait till she tells you it's time—that's my advice.

Now I need to ask you something. Sometimes I feel like I ask for a lot, and that's probably because I do, but I don't ask for things that aren't needed. If I forgot to say thank you for helping me figure out the land war, I'm sorry. Thank you. But the truth is, it hasn't helped much. I know you know what's going on, but I don't know what you're trying to do. We need your help. I think a lot of families do. I pray that you help us find a solution. I'm afraid of what might happen if the wrong man tries to solve it himself. Please help us. Amen.

ANNA

I can't believe I ever thought Danielle wanted to leave the carnival early because of her period. She can get grouchy when she has it, but it did seem like a ridiculous reason to leave. Turns out she had a lot on her mind.

I didn't get all the details, and I didn't understand everything, but I learned real quick in that waiting room that her family was in jeopardy of losing all their land to Native Americans. Of course we were also barely breathing because Danielle's grandma was in emergency surgery.

Her grandma had a heart attack. All the stress from worrying about her husband and their land mess caused a piece of plaque to break free and travel to her heart, where it got stuck. Plaque is made of cholesterol, which in an older person like Danielle's grandma could have been in her arteries for many years. Her grandma was okay with just the cholesterol, but all the stress was giving her high blood pressure, and that's what no one knew about. It was the high blood pressure and increased stress that made some of the plaque break free. When it got stuck, blood couldn't keep circulating to that area of her heart. Then she collapsed with a heart attack. I learned about all this stuff with Nurse Rose at the center. Mom and I had helped with several patients who were recovering from heart attacks.

The doctors had to cut Danielle's grandmother open to fix her heart so that the blood could circulate. That's called a bypass. Her grandmother made it—but she still had a long road to recovery. That was where I came in.

Mom and I were the in-home care people for Danielle's grandma. We helped her do rehab exercises, keeping a careful eye on how she handled walking around. Did she get short of breath? How did her breathing sound and how well did she recover from any exercise? Of course there were also some trained nurses (Nurse Rose and others) who came once or twice a week to check her blood pressure and to clean her incision. Danielle's grandma also had to go to the doctor every so often to get checked. But on a daily basis, it was Mom and I who helped the most. We even kept her house in order by doing the laundry and the cleaning.

Danielle and her mother took care of the meals. Danielle checked in on her grandma a lot (everyone did), but she also did her share of farmwork by carrying out her grandma's jobs. She tended to the garden and mowed the lawns, and like I already mentioned, she had a lot to do with preparing the meals.

Her grandpa, on the other hand, still walked around with a heavy heart, if not a sick one. His wife's close call had taken a toll on him. And then to have a Native American doctor to thank for saving her in the midst of a messy land ordeal—which didn't seem to be getting figured out any time soon—that ate at him too.

Well, Danielle's grandpa came into the house for a drink one afternoon, and it was her grandma who set him straight. "Alfred," she said. "You need to stop this moping around if you expect me to get any better. I can't keep worrying about you while I'm trying to make my heart strong again."

He looked at me and said, "I guess you got her feeling better. She's back to nagging at me." Then there came a slight smile. The first I'd seen from him. He put his empty glass down, grabbed his hat, and headed back out the door. I followed him.

I stood behind him on the porch, looking out over the farm. I thought of our Collaborative Classroom friend James and his words to Peter last year. "She's right, sir," I said. "None of it's your fault."

Believe me, saying that took all the courage I could muster up. Her grandpa never turned around to look at me. He wiped at his face with the handkerchief from his pocket, then stepped off the porch and returned to the business of his farm.

I headed back into the house, where my mom and Danielle's grandma sat at the kitchen table. That was when Danielle's grandma said something that I know my mom felt in her heart, 'cause I sure felt it in mine.

"You know," her grandma began, "there was a time when I was convinced the devil himself had set the two of you upon this family . . . but how wrong I was. I know now that our God sent us some angels instead."

I was so happy and relieved to finally have Grandma Evelyn on my side.

Alexia

A few days after Danielle's grandma had a heart attack, I was sitting in a booth doing my homework at the restaurant. It was about an hour before closing time. Mom and Vincent were in the back. Mom was getting whatever she needed for the last table she was waiting, and Vincent was beginning to clean up for the night. The door opened, but I didn't look to see who it was until they sat across from me.

"Hey, Little Brat," Reena said.

"Hi, Lexie," Lisa said.

"Hey," I said back. Then like, the dumbest thing came out of my mouth. "Where's Brandon?" I could have kicked myself.

"He's getting help." Lisa leaned forward. "Thanks to you."

I didn't say anything, but I know I looked surprised.

"After his car rampage—the one you and that boy caused. We saw you running away from the scene," Lisa said.

"Hand in hand, I might add," Reena said. "Did you kiss him?"

"Reena, stop for a sec," Lisa said. "Let me finish. The officer at the carnival took Brandon into custody. It was clear he'd been drinking. Now he's enrolled in an alcohol and substance abuse program that will hopefully help him get a fresh start."

I smiled.

"We wanted to get him help," Lisa said, "but we didn't know how to go about it. He changed so quickly after his injury. I felt bad for him so I went along with whatever he did."

"I know," I said, thinking of Mom and Dad. I understood how hard it was to get control in that situation. And how it took courage.

"Did you kiss him?" Reena asked again.

"Of course," I said. "And not like a kindergartner."

Reena laughed.

I was telling the truth. I didn't do one of those little pecks like Margaret tried, and like Peter thought we were going to do. I was a good kisser. Peter, on the other hand, needed practice.

"We'd better go. My mom is waiting for us outside," Lisa said. "See ya."

"See ya," I said back.

"Don't worry, Little Brat. If I see you in the halls next year, I'll be sure to talk to you," Reena said.

I smiled. "Sounds good."

Then they turned and walked out.

Mom came over just as they were leaving and slid in next to me. She asked about "those girls," so I explained everything to her. Heart-to-heart talks like this were still new for us, but I loved them. Did I owe getting my mother back to my friends, my time at the hangout, or Teach? Whatever the reason, it didn't matter. I just knew I wasn't ever giving her back. I leaned over and hugged Mom. We stayed like that until Vincent came out of the kitchen and hit us with one of his corny jokes.

"Can you believe they just discovered diarrhea is genetic?" he announced as he walked across the restaurant floor. Mom and I looked at each other with scrunched-up faces. "That's right," he said. "They say it runs in your *jeans*."

Vincent bent over laughing and slapped his knee. And you know what, I was laughing too.

Jessica

JESSICA VO

We were over the hurdle. Danielle's grandma had made it. The only thing left for us was a happy ending, which meant graduation and a wedding—but of course, there were still a few surprises.

As the end of the school year approaches, most teachers tend to lighten up. You might not get as much homework and you might get a little more free time in the classroom. There's still work to be done, but it's not as serious. Everyone is counting down the days.

None of this was the case for our class. Not one of us was anxious for the school year to be over, including Mr. Terupt. He wanted to teach us all as much as he could before his time was up. So instead of kicking back and relaxing, he told us we had another book to read. Another book that he wanted to bring alive for us. I knew this meant connections.

There was no complaining. The only downside any of us saw in having another project at this time of year was that it would make the few remaining days go by faster. When you're bored, the days creep by, but when you're participating in any of Mr. Terupt's projects, time flies.

FADE IN: Classroom.

MR. TERUPT

I have a bag of crayons here.

MR. TERUPT holds a brown paper bag for all to see.

MR. TERUPT

I'm going to come around so that each of you can reach in and take one. No peeking. I'll explain what this is for after everyone picks.

Camera follows MR. TERUPT around as each student selects from the bag. The crayons are all different sizes. Some with paper, some without. Some broken and others brand-new. But all are either red or blue.

MR. TERUPT
(holding up a book)

Okay gang, here is the next class novel. *The Whipping Boy* by Sid Fleischman. It's another older book and another Newbery Medal winner. Do any of you know what a whipping boy is?

PETER

A boy who gets whipped.

LEXIE

Duh!

We hear giggling throughout the class. PETER and LEXIE are back to normal after a night of romance.

MR. TERUPT

Yes, a whipping boy is a boy who gets whipped. For what?

PETER

Naughty bathroom behavior.

LEXIE

Ha-ha!

MR. TERUPT

Yes, for naughty behavior. But whose?

Classroom grows quiet. We see many puzzled expressions.

MR. TERUPT

Good. Now I've got your attention. Believe it or not, some royal households of past centuries kept whipping boys to suffer the punishments for a misbehaving prince.

JESSICA
(appalled)
You mean the prince misbehaved and then some other boy
was whipped for it!

MR. TERUPT
Yes, that's exactly the case. The other boy wasn't royalty, but
some low-level peasant. As Mr. Fleischman will refer to him,
"a street rat."

ANNA
But that's not fair.

MR. TERUPT grows a big smile. We watch him unroll a worn
piece of parchment. He clears his throat and then reads.

MR. TERUPT
A new Snow Hill School law. It has been declared, on this
twenty-sixth day of May, that those of you holding blue crayons are hereby considered royalty, and those of you holding
red crayons are whipping boys. Royalty will enjoy extra recess while whipping boys will bear the burden of extra classroom work. Royalty will enjoy Field Day, and whipping boys
will not.

PETER slams his desk and jumps to his feet in an outrage, the
red crayon still in his hand.

PETER
You can't do that! It's not fair!

MR. TERUPT
(continuing to read from the parchment)
It is in this spirit that we will connect with Mr. Fleischman's story and bring it to life. Signed, Mary Williams, queen of Snow Hill School, and William Terupt, knight in shining armor.

MR. TERUPT tacks the new law to the classroom bulletin board. Then he turns around to face the class, specifically PETER.

MR. TERUPT
So you see, Peter, I didn't do anything. This new law comes from our queen, and that's just the way it is.

MR. TERUPT begins passing out the novels.

MR. TERUPT
Here are your books. Once you have your copy you may begin. As always, be sure to record all your important thinking and questioning in your journal. Happy reading.

JEFFREY
(in a grumbling voice)
Peter's right. This isn't fair.

MR. TERUPT walks back to his seat without saying anything else, but he has a smile that he can't hide.

FADE OUT.

JESSICA VO

At lunch, I felt bad when I overheard Jeffrey telling Peter that he hated "the royalty." That was when Luke got up from our table and threw his food and blue crayon in the trash. Danielle and Anna had selected red crayons, so they had to stay inside for recess. I didn't have much fun without them. I just felt terrible. And I couldn't believe they were going to miss out on Field Day. I agreed. It wasn't fair. But why did Mr. Terupt only smile any time that was mentioned?

Jeffrey

Field Day was something Peter and I had been looking forward to for over a month. Ever since Terupt had told us wrestling was going to be part of it. But then he went ahead and robbed us of that opportunity with some new law that he and Mrs. Williams thought up. I was ripped. As soon as everything was going okay in my life, things got screwed up. It wasn't fair.

I went home and complained to Mom about the stupid law. Mom was going to be volunteering at Field Day, and she planned to bring Asher with her so everyone could see him. I wanted to be there for that. I wanted Anna to see him. I told Mom that the stupid law wasn't fair.

"A lot in life isn't," Mom said. "You've known that for a long time."

I didn't know what to say. Mom was right. Was that what

Terupt wanted us to get out of this experience? That life wasn't fair? That's a good lesson, but I didn't need to miss Field Day to understand it. I made up my mind to tell Terupt just that, but I never got a chance.

He got us started reading that stupid book first thing the next morning, and by the time we stopped, the roles in the book had reversed. Something crazy happens in the story so that the whipping boy becomes the prince and the prince becomes the whipping boy. So Terupt reversed the roles in our classroom. Suddenly, I was royalty. I had the privilege of recess that day, while the former royalty did not. And I was going to be able to participate in Field Day!

My excitement didn't last very long. By the end of recess I was feeling bad for the kids stuck inside. And I felt even worse about them missing Field Day. It sucked being one of the peasants, but I think it was easier being one of them than it was being stuck as royalty. I know that might sound weird, but it's true. It stunk for these guys to suddenly be peasants, but that was just the way it was going to be.

I hoped something would happen in the book to fix everything once and for all. That was the only chance I saw for change. But Peter thought differently. He wasn't waiting on the book. He decided to make a move, and once he did, it was easy for the rest of us to follow.

LUKE

Supposedly, I was a hero for helping Danielle's grandma at the carnival. Usually I want to be recognized as the best, but not this time. Lots of people helped. I just did what I'd learned to do. What Peter did during Mr. Terupt's *Whipping Boy* project was a lot more courageous.

It was Field Day. We came to school that morning with half our class still deemed royalty and the other half peasants. There wasn't much of the story left for us to read, so Mr. Terupt had us finish it before Field Day got started. This was where Peter stepped in. We were all seated and ready to start reading when he stood up.

"I'd like to say something," he said. "Last year I spent a chunk of time alone and feeling helpless. I remember what that was like—it stunk! And now a bunch of you are stuck as peasants and there's nothing you can do about it. You're helpless. I don't like it and I don't feel good about it. I don't care if I'm supposed to be royalty. I'm not going out to Field Day if you can't come with us."

Peter sat down. His voice was shaking and beginning to crack by the time he finished.

"Peter's right," Jeffrey said, standing up. "I'm not going out unless everyone comes either." He sat back down.

Wendy was next. She stood up and did the same. Then Marty. Then Nick. By the time the protesting stopped, all the royalty had joined Peter.

Now you know why I said Peter was the hero.

We waited for Mr. Terupt's response.

"Can any of you tell me what lessons I was hoping you'd get out of this book and our class law?"

"Yeah," Jeffrey said. "Life isn't fair."

"That's right," Mr. Terupt said. "We've had plenty of experience with that truth already, but let this be a final reminder. You need to keep working hard and stick together. Your hard work and friendships will help you through good and bad. The exchange program provided you with opportunities to abandon each other, but you didn't. Next year and beyond will provide the same opportunities, and I hope you remain together then. Now, what's the last lesson learned that Peter just showed us?"

Jessica spoke up. "That when we see unfair situations or injustices in our world, it's up to us to do something about them. Remaining silent when we don't agree with what's happening does no good. That only allows the unfair situation to continue."

"Spoken beautifully, Jessica. I couldn't have said it any better myself. And I definitely couldn't have showed you what to do any better than Peter did. Thank you, Peter."

We finished the book after that. Mr. Terupt actually read it aloud and we followed along. It has a great ending because the two boys become best friends and both enjoy being free—there is no more whipping boy! That meant there were no longer peasants in our classroom, and we were all allowed to attend Field Day! It was a moment of celebration.

To be honest, I really don't remember much from this year's Field Day. But I'll always remember Mr. Terupt's *Whipping Boy* twist leading up to the day. And I'll always remember Peter's heroic stand.

CONCLUSION
—Peter was the hero.

Detective Luke

Peter

Jeffrey and I got to wrestle at Field Day, and we were easily the best. It was fun to show off our stuff. Everyone thought we were amazing. Jeffrey's new little brother, Asher, sat by the side of the mat bouncing up and down and clapping the whole time.

I could tell you all about the moves I hit and how nasty I looked doing them, but there was something else more important than that. Our guest referee was a high school kid volunteering his time—Middle-Finger Boy. I remembered him well. Lexie filled me in on Brandon being a wrestler and how he missed competing this past season because of an injury. Coach Terupt knew the story and wanted to help the kid, despite his middle finger. No surprise there.

Brandon turned out to be pretty cool. He showed me and Jeffrey a couple of nice moves at the end of the day. Something told me I'd be seeing more of him at my wrestling practices, and I was good with that.

PART THREE

june

Jeffrey

I sat on that stage at graduation looking out at all the people. I had a family sitting down in the audience. It's hard to explain how much that meant to me. Last year, I wouldn't have been able to say that. I spent time in a silent house with a mom and dad who barely spoke to each other or to me. I know what I've got now, and I don't ever want to lose it.

Asher is already ten months old. He's crawling all over the place, and he can stand up when he has something to grab on to. I've been teaching him a wrestling stance. He's got a good one.

Dad and I had such a good time building the bookcase that we've decided to tackle another project together. This one is a little bigger.

After Michael passed away Mom couldn't stand to see

his empty bedroom. Closing the door didn't help. His room was still there, haunting her. I don't think Dad and I liked it any better. So we moved to a house with one less bedroom, but now we have a need of another—Asher's. Dad and I are going to build it. We're making our house a home.

Danielle

Some people say that when you have a brush with death, or if someone you care for deeply has a brush with death, then that can lead you to finding God. I'd known God for a long time, but I won't deny that Grandma's close call brought me even closer to Him. Everything around me took on a religious feel.

Take Peter, for example. He was Moses. Moses was royalty and chose to join the slaves. Didn't Peter do that when we read *The Whipping Boy*? Yes. He was one of our angels. And so was Luke, for helping my grandmother. And Mr. Terupt. And Anna, for also helping Grandma—in many ways. And Jeffrey, for saving Asher. Angels were all around us and among us. Jessica was the next one I spotted.

She stood at the podium as our class orator. Every year, at graduation ceremonies across the land, select students gave talks about their memories and words of encouragement for the future. Each of the sixth-grade classes at Snow Hill School chose such a speaker. We couldn't have picked a better person from our class than Jessica.

"I titled my speech *Time with Mr. Terupt*," she said.

But what I heard was, "A reading from the Gospel according to Mr. Terupt." That was how special I knew her words were going to be, and everyone else in the audience knew it too.

Dear God,

Thank you! I'm praying just to give thanks—for surrounding me with such wonderful people. I can see all the angels now. Also for giving me Grandma back. But you've done more than that. I can see now that one of my longtime prayers is being answered. Graduation is sort of a big deal—even for sixth graders, so that means dressing up. When I went to put on my favorite pair of dress pants I couldn't believe it. Another pair of high-waters. Once dress pants, now capris. And they were loose around my waist! "You'll thin out," Mom has always told me. I guess it's time. Maybe this period thing isn't all bad after all. Thank you. Amen.

Jessica

FADE IN: SIXTH-GRADE GRADUATION. Rows of chairs line the gymnasium floor, none empty. People stand against the padded walls along the sides and back of the room. Large industrial-sized fans are stationed by the doors and help circulate air through the crowd on this hot and sticky afternoon. All sixth graders sit in folding chairs on the stage, arranged in alphabetical order by last name. MRS. WILLIAMS sits with the graduates, and the teachers sit off to the side. There is a podium for each speaker to use and there are balloons tied in various locations all around the room. Parents, relatives, and friends are in attendance, many of them with bunches of flowers to give to their special student.

CUT TO: JESSICA standing at the podium. She opens her speech and presses it flat, running her hand over the crease. Her eyes survey the audience.

Long ago my father taught me a trick for whenever you found yourself standing in front of a large group of people. This trick was important in his line of work as a play director—he passed it on to many of his actors. It was a way to rid a person of stage fright. As I looked out over the sea of people before me, I pictured them all naked. That's it—that's the trick. And it works! Once all those people in front of you are naked they look pretty ridiculous, and then talking to them is a cinch. The only problem I had was that all the people in the audience were parents and grandparents—it was a tad gross seeing all these old farts (as Peter would say) naked.

JESSICA gives a small, I-see-you smile. Then she takes a deep breath and begins.

JESSICA

In our class, we recently had an experience with a book titled *The Whipping Boy*. All schools try very hard to make everything in their classrooms fair. I wonder, do young people grow up expecting life to be the same? One of the things our teacher, Mr. Terupt, made apparent for us while reading *The Whipping Boy* is that life is not always fair. If we remind ourselves of all that we've been through in the past two years, then we find other examples proving the same point. We've learned how to combat unfairness in life by spreading goodness, and to act when we see something that's not right.

Those of us who became royalty during our *Whipping Boy* experience did not feel good about the treatment our peasant friends received. In fact, in many ways it was easier to be an angry peasant than it was to be guilty royalty. Staying quiet and allowing unjust situations to occur is as bad as creating them.

In my time at Snow Hill School, I've grown to believe that things happen for a reason. And though I am not always able to identify those reasons, still I hold on to this belief. Most kids move through life without experiencing what we've encountered over the past two years. That's what makes us special. We are moving on to the next chapter in our lives, with experiences beyond our years. These experiences make us unique, they've happened for a reason, and I think one of those reasons is so we can go forward and try to do for others what our teachers have done for us.

I will never forget my time here, and I know you won't either. Thank you.

JESSICA looks out over the audience. We see people throughout the gym beginning to stand as the room fills with applause. JESSICA smiles and gives a small wave, then returns to her seat. MR. TERUPT is there and gives her a hug before she sits down.

MR. TERUPT
(whispering in Jessica's ear)
You were terrific.

JESSICA
So were you.

MRS. WILLIAMS stands and walks to the podium. JESSICA and MR. TERUPT sit. The audience grows quiet again and MRS. WILLIAMS continues with the ceremony.

MRS. WILLIAMS

Thank you to each of our class orators. Your speeches were beautiful. You've left no doubt about why you were chosen to speak. Your words will not be forgotten. Thank you.

Before we conclude our ceremony we have one last presentation. Each year a committee of Snow Hill School faculty and staff convene to select one student to receive the Snow Hill School Prize. This is an award given to a graduating sixth grader who has made an everlasting mark on our school. This year the award is being given to a student who we feel has bettered herself, has bettered the people around her, and whose quiet presence has graced Snow Hill School. This year's Snow Hill School Prize is awarded to Anna Adams.

Once again, we see everyone in the gymnasium rise to their feet in applause—this time for ANNA. ANNA walks to the podium and gives MRS. WILLIAMS a ginormous hug. Then she turns and gives MR. TERUPT an even bigger one.

JESSICA VO

Isn't it funny that all of us—meaning his students—would say Mr. Terupt has made the magic. But Mr. Terupt would say it's us, his students, who have done the amazing work. I feel so good inside to see Anna getting this award, and by the sound of the applause and wild cheering, I know everyone else feels exactly the same.

FADE OUT.

LUKE

As I sat on the stage at graduation and watched Anna win the Snow Hill School Prize, I remembered the time Peter won the homework pass for having correctly estimated the number of links in our final paper chain. I wanted to kill him after that, especially for the way he rubbed it in my face.

But I didn't feel like that with Anna. For the first time in my life I was happy to see someone else win. Okay, maybe a tiny piece of me did wish it was me getting the award, but I really did feel very happy for Anna. She's the sweetest person I know. She didn't even want to harm her plant last year during our science unit, never mind ever hurt another person. Anna was a great pick for the prize.

Once the ceremony was complete, my mind immediately moved to the next big event. We were now in the final phase before the wedding. I was anxious to test my last hypothesis. And this was a one-shot deal. We weren't retesting.

Hypothesis
—If all goes as planned, then there will be a wonderful wedding and terrific ending.

Detective Luke

Peter

After graduation, there was a big outdoor reception with drinks and little snacks. It was a time for people to talk and celebrate and congratulate the graduates, but the only person I wanted to talk to was my father.

My mom and dad both made it for my graduation. As busy as they always were, they never missed the big events. Miss Catalina was also present, and my brother, Richard. He was home from school for the summer.

We sat under a tent, drinking lemonade and iced tea and eating cookies.

"Well, Pete," Richard said, "now that you're done with this dump, you get to go to Riverway." Richard's always been a moron, but you couldn't blame him much this time since he'd been away at school. How was he supposed to know I loved Snow Hill School and didn't want to go to Riverway?

That's right—I had made my mind up. I'd been back and forth about the decision, thinking I needed to fail to be with Mr. T, but now I knew I didn't want to flunk sixth grade. But I did want to stay in Snow Hill because I wanted to be with my friends.

"I won't be going to Riverway," I said.

"What?!" Richard yelped. He almost choked on his cookie.

"I don't want to go to Riverway. I want to stay here with my friends."

"Pete, you'll make new friends at Riverway. I worried about the same thing. Trust me, you'll love it way more than any local junior high school," Richard said. "And way more than this dump."

"Stop calling it that!" I snapped. "This place isn't a dump. And the friends I've made here aren't the kind of friends you just let go. We've been through way too much together."

"Pete—"

"That's enough, Richard," my father said. "Listen to your brother for once—I finally did." Dad looked at me. "This does not come as a surprise to your mother and me," he said. "Once we started paying attention we saw that your friend-ships here definitely are special. We understand why you don't want to leave."

"You do?!" I was shocked. I never expected my mother or my father to understand. Sure, they'd given me time to think about my decision, but not in a million years did I think they'd be okay with me not choosing Riverway. My plan to fail had failed, but things were working out. I was going to move on with my friends. I was relieved to know I'd be with Luke and Jeffrey, and everyone else—even Lexie and her unique wardrobe, her fast moves and salty tongue, and her rotten farts that I'd somehow get blamed for.

Last year I suddenly felt way lighter when Mr. T took the weight of the accident off my shoulders with his hug. This year my father made me feel that all over again when he told me I could stay.

The only thing left for me to do now was throw one heck of a party for Mr. T and Ms. Newberry.

Alexia

It was close to wedding time. Mom was in the school kitchen with Vincent, putting the final touches on some of the hors d'oeuvres and prepping the main dishes. I planned to help, but I wanted to see Teach and Ms. Newberry get married first. I was so anxious. Maybe that was why I had to pee again—out of excitement.

"Danielle, I've got to use the bathroom. C'mon."

"Again?!" she said.

Danielle was nervous and excited too. She needed to keep busy, so I made her come with me. I sat on the toilet while Danielle waited by the sinks. When I finished I bent forward to pull my underwear back up and saw the red spot. I jumped off the toilet.

"I got it!" I yelled. "I got it! Thank you, Margaret."

"Got what?" Danielle asked from outside my stall. "Who's Margaret?"

I fixed my dress and rushed out. "My period," I said. "I just got my period!"

Danielle gave me a big hug. "Congratulations," she said. "You're officially a woman, though I think you've been one for a long while already."

"Thanks," I said. I stepped back and looked at her. "I hope my period does for me what it's done for you. I know there are all kinds of changes that come along with it."

Danielle smiled. I hoped my words sounded nice, because I sure meant them that way. Danielle was totally getting taller and thinner.

"Thanks, Lexie," Danielle said. "You don't need your period to look great, though. You're already beautiful. You always have been."

We hugged again, but this time I was crying. Maybe it was my period making me emotional.

"I need to put a pad on," I said, suddenly realizing I forgot to do that in the stall. I'd been too excited.

"You have one?" Danielle asked.

"Of course," I said. "I've been waiting a long time for this day." I pulled a pad out of my purse and held it up, smiling. Mine was your normal winged pad, not one of those crazy old-fashioned things that Margaret mentioned where you had to wear a belt.

Once I was all situated, we left the bathroom and headed back outside. The wedding was ready to start any minute. We hurried across the grass. Before we got to our seats, I stopped Danielle.

"Do these look bigger now?" I asked her, readjusting my top.

I didn't see Peter coming until he was right next to us. He must have been on his way back from the boys' bathroom.

"Nah," he said. "They still look like a couple of mosquito bites."

I slugged him good in the arm, and then all three of us were laughing.

The music for the ceremony started, so we hurried to our seats. I was going to miss Teach a lot. I already did. But I was so happy to have my friends going with me to seventh grade, even Peter—especially Peter. I loved picking on him. And he definitely needed more kissing practice.

I was ready for next year. Look out, future, I'm a woman now!

Danielle

The weather was perfect. The wedding was perfect. Mom and Grandma cried through the ceremony, and so did Mrs. Williams. Ms. Newberry looked gorgeous in her wedding dress. She and Mr. Terupt looked so happy, and so in love. Anna and I squeezed each other in a big hug after Mr. Terupt kissed his bride.

The food Lexie's mother and Vincent cooked (with Lexie's help) was delicious. The flowers and centerpieces were beautiful, and Peter did an unbelievable job DJing. The temporary dance floor that Luke wanted stayed busy all afternoon and into the evening. But my favorite part of the reception was the wedding cake. Grandma made it. She had made wedding cakes for friends before, so she insisted on making this one despite all our objections. We were concerned she was doing too much too soon after her heart attack, but she wouldn't hear it. You know what they say—if you can't beat 'em, join 'em. So I did. I helped her make it. Grandma mixed in some spices that bit you when you took a taste. According to Grandma, this was the cake's way of making sure you were paying attention before the moistness and sweet flavors took over your mouth. It was a tower cake with bride and groom cows on the top. That was the only decoration piece Grandma could find in the house, so that was what we used. I liked it. I knew it would make Mr. and Mrs. Terupt smile, too.

Grandma and I found a way to talk about the land struggle in a calm manner while we made the wedding cake. As far as Grandma could tell, "and your grandfather would tell you the same," she said, "this land dispute looks like it's going to be in the hands of lawyers for years. That's great for your grandfather and me, but that's never been our concern. We just want to make sure the family's going to be okay after we're gone."

"We will be," I said.

"I know you will, and so does your grandfather. You're growing into a strong young woman, much tougher and wiser than I ever was at your age," Grandma said. "We know you'll be able to handle yourself."

I smiled. There wasn't anything that made me feel as good as Grandma's praise. *Thank you for giving her back to us, God. I might be tough, but I'm not ready to live without her yet.*

"And Charlie's got himself a wonderful woman now. He ought to be the next getting married," Grandma said.

I smiled even bigger. I couldn't wait to tell Anna what Grandma had said.

Dear God,

I know I need to trust you. That's what faith is all about. Grandma and I figure her doctor being Native American is your way of telling us that they aren't bad people. Please forgive me for thinking all those terrible things without knowing anything about them. Grandma's right, Charlie and I will be able to handle ourselves. I trust you. Amen.

ANNA

It wasn't just the way Mr. Terupt looked at Ms. Newberry, but the way she looked at him too. They had a way of saying "I love you" with their eyes. And that was exactly what they were saying while holding each other's hands and gaze during their vows. Mr. Terupt gave Ms. Newberry a very romantic kiss and then they were announced as Mr. and Mrs. Terupt.

Danielle and I gave each other a big hug. There were hugs and handshakes going on all around us. Then it was time for the reception. Danielle and I couldn't wait—we had a secret plan up our sleeves.

I had never won anything before the Snow Hill School Prize. To be honest, I still can't believe I won it. I remember hugging Mr. Terupt after receiving the award.

"The world would be a beautiful place if it were full of

Annas," he whispered to me. "You've helped us all by being nothing but good."

I squeezed him. The world would be a beautiful place if it were full of Mr. Terupts, I thought. As I took my seat and looked out over the audience, I saw a couple of people left for me to help. That was where the secret plan came in.

During the wedding reception all the single girls would gather on the dance floor, ready for the bride to throw her bouquet over her shoulder. The girl who caught the bouquet was supposed to be the next to get married. After Grandma Evelyn gave my mom and Charlie her stamp of approval, Danielle and I knew we had to get that bouquet into my mom's hands. With some sneaky pushing and maneuvering, we jockeyed my mom front and center on the dance floor.

"On three," Peter announced with his DJing microphone. "One-two-three."

The flowers sailed through the air, and Danielle and I used our bodies to keep everyone else away. Mr. Terupt told us afterward that we looked like a couple of basketball players boxing out for a rebound—whatever that meant. The important thing was, Mom caught the bouquet. When she looked up she smiled at Charlie. He smiled back and shrugged. Danielle and I hurried off and gave Grandma Evelyn a high five. She was the one who helped us hatch the scheme.

What a wonderful ending! I couldn't wait to plan the next wedding.

Mr. Terupt gave me a wink from across the dance floor. He knew I liked playing matchmaker, and I was pretty good at it too.

Peter

"You may kiss the bride."

Mr. T planted a big one on Ms. Newberry. It was long, but nothing crazy. I bet Ms. Newberry wouldn't have tasted like salt. She looked beautiful. Mr. T was a lucky man.

I threw one heck of a party. Just like Mr. T wanted. I kept the music pumping and the dancing never slowed. There was one song that everyone will remember—"It Had to Be You" by Harry Connick Jr. I played it at Mr. T's request. Mr. and Mrs. Terupt brought down the house with a swing dance that'll never be forgotten. After that everyone stayed on the floor and danced the night away, including me. I danced with the foxy Mrs. Terupt. Miss Catalina. Mrs. Williams! My mom! And yes, Lexie.

"It's time, Peter," Mr. T said. He was standing beside me at the DJing table, smiling as he looked at all the people having fun. "It's time to forgive yourself."

I turned and grabbed him in a hug. "Okay," I said. "Okay." He squeezed me harder.

It was a shame the night had to end, but I knew there were more good times ahead. The lovely Mr. and Mrs. Terupt wouldn't be far away, and I would be with my friends. As I walked down new school halls next year, I wouldn't be remembering the worst thing I'd ever done, but the best days of my life—these past two years with Mr. T.

NOTED

Jeffrey

I've heard Jessica talk about happy endings before. She loves them. After Mr. and Mrs. Terupt showed everyone how to let loose with their big-time swing dance, I looked across the dance floor and saw Dad spinning and twirling Mom. Then I looked down and saw Asher bending his knees and bouncing. No one had a bigger smile or felt better than me at that moment. It was a happy ending—a very happy ending.

LUKE

Many boys dream of being like their favorite football or baseball player when they grow up. Others of being president. I used to think I wanted to be an astronaut. Then a chemist. Then a detective.

Conclusion
—I have no idea what I'll end up doing, but I do know I want to be like Mr. Terupt.

Mr. Luke Bennett

Jessica

I love to read. I've read stories upon stories. For whatever reason, fairy tales have always been my least favorite, yet I still can't help but feel that we've been part of one. Our valiant prince, Mr. Terupt, fought for his life along the way, spread good to all his kingdom, and eventually found true love with his beautiful princess, Ms. Newberry. And yes, now they'll live happily ever after.

FADE OUT.

ACKNOWLEDGMENTS

Many people have helped along the way. I give my sincere thanks to all of you, no matter how small a part you might think you've played.

To all the teachers and librarians who have embraced Mr. Terupt and his students.

To the booksellers who have put Mr. Terupt in the hands of parents and kids.

To Sarah and Noah Burstein for being excellent readers.

To John Irving for your incredible wisdom and true friendship. You're a great coach.

To Paul Fedorko for your time and continued work on my behalf.

To Françoise Bui for your insightful comments and feedback, for your honesty, and for all your hard work.

To all my friends and family, who have not only done plenty to spread the word, but have provided rock-solid support and positive encouragement. I can't thank you enough.

To my beautiful daughters, Emma, Lily, and Anya, who allow me to find time to write by not getting up as early as me. To Emma for being my first reader, and to Lily and Anya, who I know are right behind their big sister. And to my faithful dog, Jake, who has me getting up even earlier as he gets older and can't hold it all night long. You make sure I get out of bed.

And lastly, to Beth, who does it all. Thank you. I love you.

ABOUT THE AUTHOR

ROB BUYEA taught third and fourth graders in Bethany, Connecticut, for six years before moving to Massachusetts, where he lives with his wife and three daughters. He teaches biology and coaches wrestling at Northfield Mount Hermon School. *Because of Mr. Terupt,* his first novel and the companion to *Mr. Terupt Falls Again,* was selected as an E. B. White Read-Aloud Honor Book and a Cybils Honor Book and has been named to numerous state award lists. Rob spends his summers at Cape Cod enjoying family adventures, entertaining friends, and writing. You can visit him at robbuyea.com.